PRAISE FOR
THE TEMPTATION SAGA

Tempting DUSTY

THE TEMPTATION SAGA
BOOK ONE

WATERHOUSE PRESS

Tempting

DUSTY

THE TEMPTATION SAGA
BOOK ONE

This one is a book of my heart, and it's for my fans. Thank you so much for reading! You've helped make my dream come true. And in memory of the real Zach and Dusty.

PROLOGUE

"Come on, Sam. Papa says it's time to go." Dusty O'Donovan tugged at her brother's sleeve. The Colorado heat made her sweat, and she pushed her red-gold hair out of her face.

"Geez, Dusty, can you give me a minute?"

"Yeah, twerp." Chad McCray nodded. "We're sealing our pact. We're blood brothers now." He held up his hand and a trickle of crimson oozed down his palm.

Dusty looked away, disgusted. She focused on the mountains. She loved the giant peaks, how they looked dark blue from here but turned miraculously green as Papa drove closer. She loved the pine trees that grew tall and skinny, trying to reach the sunlight through the thick evergreen brush. She loved the reddish-brown rock that made faces at her if she stared hard enough. Would there be mountains where they were going?

She turned back to pull on Sam's sleeve again. Redness dribbled on her brother's hand. Her mouth filled with saliva, and queasiness erupted in her throat.

She hated the sight of blood. Not because she was a baby. Heck, she carried snakes and lizards in her pockets. No, she hated it because blood was killing her mama. Bad blood. Something about the cells that were white, though Dusty didn't understand that. She had seen her mama's blood, and it was red, just like everyone else's.

This white blood murderer had a name. *Loo-kee-mee-uh.*

"You all still hangin' around?" Chad's older brother Zach loped up. At thirteen, the black-haired boy was tall and lanky, all arms and legs. He looked funny. He sounded funny too. Especially when his voice did that crackly thing.

Then he glared at her with those eyes.

"Don't, Zach."

"I'm just teasin', Gold Dust," Zach said. "You don't believe I can hurt you anymore, do you? Big girl like you ain't gonna fall for that nonsense."

"Course not." Dusty looked away anyway. Zach's eyes were creepy. One was dark brown and the other light blue. He had been teasing Dusty since she was a toddler, telling her his blue eye packed a laser that melted little girls' brains.

She turned and grasped her brother's arm. "Now, Sam."

"All right, I'm comin'. Sheesh." Sam looked sheepishly at Chad. "See ya around."

"Yeah, I guess."

"Come on, you two." The oldest of the brothers, Dallas, walked toward them. "You all have chores to do."

"Heck, you're not our pa," Chad said. "Sam's leavin' today."

"Do I look like I care? Come on now."

"I gotta go anyway," Sam said. "Come on, Dust."

When Sam grabbed her hand, Dusty looked back at the McCray brothers.

Zach, with his funny eyes, spoke. "Keep your chin up, Gold Dust. Everything'll be all right."

Dusty nodded and curled her small fingers into Sam's larger ones. As they walked toward the small house that was the only home she had ever known, she stared up at her brother. His eyes seemed sunken in his face. He looked sad.

"I'm sorry you have to leave your best friend, Sam."

"Ain't nothin'."

Dusty, young as she was, knew her ten-year-old brother would miss Chad McCray. Both were the same age, and they'd been inseparable for years.

"Come on, you two varmints," Sean-Patrick O'Donovan said, as he helped Dusty's mother, Mollie, into the white minivan. "Take a quick look through the house and see if we've missed anything, though I doubt it. Your mama here even swept the place."

"I didn't want to leave a dirty house, Sean," Mollie said.

"Christ, honey, we're leavin'. Who cares what the place looks like?"

"I do."

"But you went and tired yourself out."

"So what? I'll have nothing to do but sleep in the car for the next eight hours."

Dusty fixed her gaze on her blond-haired, blue-eyed mother, pale and weak, and wondered why sweeping the house was so important when she was obviously exhausted. Her mama, once so fresh and flushed, now had skin the color of the worn grey fence surrounding their small vegetable garden. Her arms, once firm and muscular as they held Dusty and rocked her to sleep, looked like thin tree branches, the skin hanging loosely.

Dusty stood silently while Sam entered the house and returned momentarily. "We got it all," he said.

"Good. Now you two get in the van."

Dusty scrambled into the backseat next to Sam, craned her head, and watched out the back window as the van curved out of the small driveway and up the private road leading out of McCray Landing. She took one last glance at the cozy little house, remembering her rosy-cheeked mama smiling and standing by the door, before she got sick. Then Dusty closed her eyes.

They were going to Montana to live with Mama's family. That's what Mama wanted. They no longer needed to stay near the big city of Denver, because Mama wasn't going back to the hospital.

The doctors couldn't help her anymore.

CHAPTER ONE

Seventeen years later

"He doesn't look so tough," Dusty said to Sam as she eyed El Diablo, the stud bull penned up outside the Western Stock Show grounds in Denver. She winced at the pungent aroma of dust and animals.

"No man's been able to stay on him more than two seconds, Dust," her brother said.

"He just needs a woman's touch." Dusty looked into the bull's menacing eyes. Oh, he was mad all right, but she had no doubt she could calm him. The ranchers in Montana didn't call her the Bull Whisperer for nothing.

"I don't know. I'm not sure you should try it. Papa wouldn't like it."

"Papa's dead, Sam, and you can't tell me what to do." She pierced her brother's dark gaze with her own. "Besides, the purse for riding him would save our ranch, and you know it."

"Hell, Dusty." Sam shoved his hands in his denim pockets. "I plan to win a few purses bronc busting. You don't need to worry about making money."

"I want to make the money, Sam."

"That's silly."

"No, it's not."

"Look, you don't need to feel any obligation. What happened couldn't be helped. It wasn't your fault. You know that."

"Whatever." She shrugged her shoulders and turned back to the bull. "Besides, if I ride old Diablo here, I can make five hundred thousand dollars in eight seconds. That's"—she did some rapid calculations in her head—"two hundred and twenty-five million dollars an hour. Can you beat that?" She grinned, raising her eyebrows.

"Your math wizardry is annoying, Dust. Always has been. And yeah, I might be able to come away from this rodeo with half a mill, though I won't do it in eight seconds. Besides, Diablo's owner will never let a woman ride him."

"Who's his owner? I haven't had a chance to look through the program yet."

"Zach McCray."

"No fooling?" Dusty smiled as she remembered the lanky teenager with the odd-colored eyes. Yes, he had tormented her, but he had been kind that last day when the O'Donovans left for Montana. At thirteen, Zach had no doubt understood the magnitude of Mollie's illness much better than Dusty. "I figured the McCrays would be here. Think they'll remember us?"

"Sure. Chad and I are blood brothers." Sam held up his palm. "Seriously, though, they may not. Ranch hands come and go all the time around a place as big as McCray Landing."

"It's Sam O'Donovan!"

Dusty turned toward the deep, resonating voice. A tall broad man with a tousled shock of brown hair ambled toward them.

"Chad? I'll be damned. It *is* you." Sam held out his hand. "We were just talking about you, wondering if you'd remember us."

"A man doesn't forget his first and only blood brother."

Chad slapped Sam on the back. "And is this the little twerp?"

"Yeah, it's me, Chad." Dusty held out her hand.

Chad grabbed it and pulled her toward him in a big bear hug. "You sure turned out to be a pretty thing. " He turned back to Sam. "I bet you got your work cut out for you, keeping the flies out of the honey."

"Yeah, so don't get any ideas," Sam said.

Chad held up his hands in mock surrender. "Wouldn't dream of it, bro. So how are you all? I'd heard you might be back in town. I was sorry to hear about your pa."

"I didn't know the news made it down here," Sam said.

"Yeah, there was a write up in the Bakersville Gazette. The old lady who runs it always kept a list of the hands hired at the nearby ranches. Once she discovered the Internet five years ago, there was no stopping her." Chad grinned. "She found every one of them. Needs a new hobby, I guess. So what are you all up to?"

"Here for the rodeo. Dusty and I are competing."

"No kidding?"

"Yep. I'm bronc busting, and Dusty's a barrel racer. And..." Sam chuckled softly.

"And what?"

"She thinks she's gonna take Diablo here for a ride."

Chad's eyes widened as he stared at Dusty. Warmth crept up her neck. Clearly her five-feet-five-inch frame didn't inspire his confidence.

"You ride bulls?"

Her facial muscles tightened. "You bet I do."

Chad let out a breathy chortle. "Good joke."

"No joke, Chad," Sam said. "She's pretty good, actually. But she's never ridden a bull as big as Diablo. She's tamed some pretty nasty studs in Montana, though never during competition."

"I hate to tell you this, Gold Dust, but this rodeo doesn't allow female bull riding."

"I'll just have to get them to change their minds then," Dusty said.

"Good luck with that," Chad said. "In fact, can I go with you? I think the whole affair might be funny."

"Fine, come along then. Who do I speak to?"

"Honey, why don't you stick to female riding? I'm sure the WPRA will be happy to hear your pleas. But this here's a *man's* rodeo."

Dusty's nostrils flared as anger seethed in her chest. "I'm as good a bull rider as any man. Tell him, Sam."

"I already told him you're good."

"But tell him what they call me back home."

"Dust—"

"Tell him, or I will!"

"They call her the Bull Whisperer. She's good, I tell you."

"Bull Whisperer?" Chad scoffed. "So you're the Cesar Millan of cattle, huh? Ain't no whisper gonna calm Diablo. Even Zach hasn't been able to ride him, and he's the best."

"Yeah, well, he hasn't seen me yet." Dusty stood with her hands on her hips, wishing her presence were more imposing. Both her brother and Chad were nearly a foot taller than she was. "I'm going to ride that bull and win that purse!"

"Seriously, Dusty," Chad said, "I was teasing you. But you can't try to ride Diablo. He'll kill you. Trust me, I know. He damn near killed me. I was out all last season recovering from injuries I got from him."

"I have a way with animals," Dusty said.

"So do I, honey."

Sam rolled his eyes, laughing. "Whatever you say, McCray."

"Hey, dogs love me," Chad said.

"I'm not surprised," Dusty said, smiling sardonically. "I'm sure you make a nice tall fire hydrant. Now tell me, who do I need to talk to about riding the bull?"

"You need to talk to me, darlin'."

Dusty shuddered at the sexy western drawl, the hot whisper of breath against the back of her neck.

"And there ain't a woman alive who can ride that bull."

CHAPTER TWO

Dusty turned to face the man behind her, and her breath caught. Tall, though not as tall as Sam or Chad—six-feet-two, maybe, in his boots. Long black hair fell to his collar in silky waves. Broad shoulders clad in a black western shirt, and lean hips hugged by snug fitting jeans. The face of a god, chiseled and perfect with a strong jawline and straight Grecian nose. Full dusky lips. *Wow.* Then she noticed his eyes. One dark brown, one light blue. Those creepy eyes. Funny, they didn't seem so bad anymore. They worked with his movie star looks. They gave him a mysterious quality, like he could see into her soul.

He was magnificent.

"Zach McCray," she said in a breathless rasp.

"I hardly recognized you, Gold Dust," he drawled, eyeing her from top to bottom.

The smolder of his unique eyes warmed her from her head to her toes, and she was convinced he was somehow dissolving her clothes with his heated gaze. Her nipples hardened against the soft fabric of her bra, and she silently thanked God she'd chosen one with padding that morning.

Dusty looked down at his feet, shod in black ostrich cowboy boots. *Expensive* black ostrich cowboy boots. Here was money. The McCray brothers no doubt owned McCray Landing now since their father had passed away a couple years ago.

"So"—she cleared her throat—"you're the man to talk to about riding this bull?" She gestured to Diablo, who snorted angrily.

"Darlin', I'll say it again. There ain't a woman alive who can ride that bull."

"I say there is," Dusty said. "And you're looking at her."

"She calls herself the Bull Whisperer, bro," Chad said.

Zach eyed her again, an amused smirk on his face. Was he looking at her chest? She crossed her arms.

"You think you can talk to bulls?"

"I don't exactly talk to them. It's not a literal whisper, Mr. McCray."

"Mr. McCray? Hell, that's my grandpa. You call me Zach, Gold Dust."

"Fine. It's not a literal whisper, Zach."

"Yeah, not a literal whisper." Chad's lips twisted into a wide leer. "She uses a flute and a turban. She's a regular bull swami."

The three men chuckled as Dusty rolled her eyes. Some things hadn't changed in seventeen years. Chad teased her as relentlessly as ever. She turned back to Zach.

"Look, I understand bulls, and they seem to understand me."

Zach rolled his head back in a sarcastic guffaw. Dusty tried not to think about his sexy golden neck and how good his pulse point would feel against her lips.

"Now that takes the cake, darlin'."

"I'm not your darling."

"Course not. Women's lib and all. I'd hate to be politically incorrect."

"Women's lib? This is the twenty-first century, not the

seventies." Dusty tapped her foot with indignation.

"Sorry, darlin'. Oops, I mean Dusty, or Miss O'Donovan."

"It's *Ms.*"

"Oh, Christ." Zach rolled his eyes.

"So can we talk about Diablo or not?"

"Not," Zach said.

"Told you, twerp." Chad smiled. "Ain't no way you get to ride Diablo."

"But I need to, for the—" Dusty stopped herself. The McCrays didn't need to know the small Montana ranch she and Sam had inherited from their grandparents was in financial trouble.

"Look, Dusty, I don't want to hear any more about this," Sam interjected. "The subject is closed."

"You're not my father, Sam," she said, keeping her temper in check. "I'll do as I please."

"Not with my bull, you won't," Zach said.

Dusty regarded the three men, all stiff as statues in their indignant stances. Perhaps she was going about this the wrong way. After all, she'd catch more flies with sugar...

"Zach," she said sweetly, "maybe we could discuss this further over a drink, or even dinner. I'm famished, and it would be fun to catch up, don't you think?"

"That sounds like a plan," Chad agreed. "Let's go for some chow. There's a great steakhouse about a mile from here."

"The lady asked me," Zach said, "and I'll take her to dinner. Alone."

"They can come too," Dusty said. "I'd love for us all to chat. It'd be fun."

Zach's eyes raked over her. "Now why would I want to share a pretty little thing like you with these two clowns?"

Dusty's cheeks heated. She couldn't think of anything to say.

"Okay, okay, bro." Chad said, backing away. "What say we go for a few beers and some chili cheese fries, Sam?"

"Uh, sure, but Dusty—"

"I'll be fine, Sam. I'll see you later at the hotel."

Her brother and his old best friend trotted off together, as if seventeen years hadn't passed.

Breathing deeply, she gathered her courage, turned to Zach, and looped her arm through his. "Shall we?"

★ ★ ★

While Dusty talked on and on about her experience handling bulls, Zach sipped his Wild Turkey and watched her. Damn, the little ragamuffin had turned into a beautiful woman. He tried to listen, really he did, but his mind kept wandering to the image of her naked on top of him. Her reddish-gold hair—his mama used to call it strawberry blond—was braided and hung to her waist in a long plait. Those big chocolate brown eyes. He could lose himself in them. Her cherry-red lips were full and sumptuous, and she had a tiny spray of freckles across her cute little nose. And her body...curves in all the right places. She filled out her stretch denim shirt, which was unbuttoned just enough to show a little cleavage. Did she have any idea how crazy she was driving him? He'd bet his life those breasts were as succulent as two juicy peaches.

"So what do you think?" he heard her ask.

"About what?"

"About what we've been talking about!" Dusty let out an audible breath. "Haven't you been listening, Zach?"

No, I've been thinking about how you'd look naked. "Of course I have. But I'm still not gonna let you ride Diablo."

"Come on. Please?"

Oh, those big brown eyes got to him. But—

"No." At her crestfallen gaze, he added, "It's for your own good, darlin'. That stud damn near killed Chad last year, and he's one of the best riders around."

"He said you're the best."

"I am. But he's a close second."

"How long have you stayed on him?"

"About three seconds."

"A couple years back one of our neighbors had a nasty one. Fireball was his name. I was able to tame him a little. I rode him for twelve seconds, Zach."

"But was he Diablo's size?"

"Well, no, but—"

"No buts, Dusty. You can't ride the bull."

"How about if I just get to know him a little."

"What do you mean?"

"Spend some time with him. Give him the chance to learn about me, respond to me."

Zach chuckled and put down the drink he had lifted to his lips. "This is a bull, darlin'. You sound like you want to take him for a picnic in the park."

"Come on. You know what I mean. Let me try. Please?"

"Too dangerous."

"So come with me. You can be our chaperone." Dusty's eyes darkened, and she curved those luscious lips into a teasing smile, clearly daring him to refuse her.

Hmm. Spend time with Dusty? Have her beautiful face and luscious body near him? He could live with that. Even with ugly Diablo as their chaperone. It was an excuse to be close to her without having to date her. Sounded like Christmas.

"Okay. You got a deal, Gold Dust."

"And stop calling me Gold Dust. You make me feel like a little kid."

"Oh, you're no little kid." He settled his gaze on her chest, caught himself, and looked up to her face. She was staring at him. He remembered how he used to scare her, telling her his blue eye would melt her brain. "Do my eyes bother you?"

She reddened, looking down at the table. "No, not at all. I...like them, actually."

"Oh?"

"They look good on you. They work. They give you a mystical look, like you can see inside a person."

Zach's insides warmed. "You're the first person who's ever said anything like that to me."

"You're kidding."

"Nope. In high school I didn't have a lot of luck with the girls. My eyes freaked them out."

Dusty looked at him, her eyes wide. "I can't believe that. Have you looked in a mirror? You're..." She flushed and looked away.

"I'm what, darlin'?" His tone was teasing, but inside he was ecstatic she found him attractive.

"Nothing."

"In college and grad school I wore a brown contact. But after that I said what the hell."

"And since then? Any problems with women?"

He gave her his best devil-may-care grin. "Nope."

Dusty looked down. "Didn't think so."

"There isn't anyone right now though." He hoped this

revelation pleased her. "I was engaged for a while, but she broke it off last year."

"Oh."

"What about you? Are there any men in your life?"

"None but my brother"—she smiled impishly—"and Diablo."

"Ah-ha, so you *do* want to date my bull," he joked.

"I'll settle for a little quality time, with you as my chaperone of course." Her giggle echoed like chimes. What a pleasant sound. She continued, "Where did you go to college?"

"Harvard."

Dusty's brown eyes widened, and her mouth dropped into an oval. "No way."

"Yeah, for undergrad and for my MBA."

"You have an MBA?"

"Don't look so surprised. We McCrays have brains, you know."

"Oh, I didn't mean to imply you didn't. But you're a rancher, Zach. A cowboy."

"McCray Landing didn't become what it was by sheer luck, darlin'. My family did it by being educated. My pa wanted me to have the best business education available."

"But getting into Harvard... It's very competitive."

"I never got less than an A in high school, and my rodeo wins helped. And my ma was a legacy."

"Laurie? I had no idea."

Zach warmed at the affection in Dusty's voice when she mentioned his mother. But of course, she would remember Laurie with affection. With her own mother wasting away, Laurie McCray had no doubt been a refreshing sight. "She's a smart cookie."

"I was too young to appreciate her intelligence, but I remember her cookies. Oatmeal raisin, always warm." Dusty closed her eyes. "How is she?"

"She's well. Still lives up at the main house. Dallas, Chad, and I each have our own places on the ranch."

"And she went to Harvard."

"Actually, no. She was the legacy, not me. She went to Vassar. But my grandpa, her pa, was a Harvard alum and set up an endowment for the undergrad college."

"Wow. And that helped you get in?"

"It didn't hurt."

Dusty sighed, smiling. "What a wonderful education you've had. I'm truly impressed, Zach."

Her praise warmed him. "Thanks." He didn't know what else to say.

"I always wanted to finish college," Dusty continued. "I only went for a year."

"Why did you quit?"

She looked away. "Circumstances."

Okay, he wouldn't push. "What did you study?"

"I like math. I'm good at it." Dusty spoke quickly and with passion. Education clearly meant a lot to her. "And I love animals. I had planned a double major in math and zoology, and then I thought I'd go to vet school."

"That's an admirable goal," Zach said.

"It's only a dream, really... What did Chad study? And Dallas?"

"Dallas studied law at Yale."

"He's a lawyer?"

"Nah, he's a rancher, just like I am."

"Then why law school?"

"Same reason I studied business. There's more to ranching than horses and cattle."

"Well sure there is, but—"

"Besides, Chad's the one with the brains for animals. He studied agriculture and animal science at Texas A&M. His grades weren't as good through high school. Never serious, that one. Too many parties and too many girls. But he has a unique way with animals."

"He said something like that to me earlier. He said dogs loved him. I teased him about it."

"We all tease him about it."

"But now I feel bad." She cocked her head. "But why should I? The two of you were teasing me about the same thing!"

"Touché, darlin'." Zach couldn't help grinning.

"This looks wonderful!" Dusty raved as their waiter set their meals down.

"Best steaks in Colorado," Zach said. "Enjoy."

"I intend to."

Dusty cut into her steak and took a large bite, making satisfied noises as she ate. Zach loved seeing a woman relish her food. Too many women these days were afraid to eat in front of a man. Not Dusty.

They chatted as they finished their meal, and Zach drove Dusty toward her hotel. She gushed all the way about his rented Jaguar—the plush leather seats, the incredible sound system, the lush interior. Zach knew he was rich, richer than Dusty's family would ever be. But he wondered, given the fact that Dusty had said she hadn't been able to finish college, if the O'Donovans were facing difficult times, more than just the day-to-day struggle of the average rancher. If her desire to ride

Diablo had less to do with proving herself, and more to do with the half mil purse he'd offered.

Halfway to her hotel, he passed the stock show grounds. The night was young yet, and he didn't want his evening with her to be over.

"You want to walk around the grounds a little?" he asked. "The vendors are here until nine."

"Uh, sure, I guess so."

"Unless you have some place to be."

"No. Nowhere but here."

"Great." He smiled at her, his heart doing a little jump at the thought of spending another hour or so in her company. Something about her...

He parked the Jag and led her into the large pavilion where the vendors were located.

"I'd rather look at the animals," Dusty said.

"They're all bedded down for the night, darlin'. I'm afraid it's only vendors tonight. But I'll buy you a corn dog."

"After that huge meal? You're kidding, right?"

"Yeah, I'm kidding. But I do need a new hat. Are you looking for anything?"

"No. I've got all I need."

"How about some bull riding spurs?"

"I don't use them. I just use my regular spurs."

Zach perused her face, stubborn and hard as granite. She sure looked serious. "Dusty, you're telling me you've been riding bulls without proper equipment?"

"Frankly, I'd prefer not to use spurs at all, but Sam insists."

"Thank God for Sam." He grabbed her hand. "Come with me."

His favorite spur vendor had set up shop in one of the

corner booths. He pulled Dusty inside.

The salesman raised his hand in greeting. "Hey, Zach. I figured I'd see you here eventually."

"How've you been, Jay?"

"Can't complain."

"This is Dusty," Zach said. "Dusty, Jay Ray."

"Jay Ray?"

"Born and bred," Jay said. "What can I do for you all this evening?"

"We need to set her up with some bull riding spurs."

"Zach, no..."

"My treat, darlin'."

"But I don't like to use spurs with bulls. How's an animal supposed to trust me if I hurt him?"

Jay chuckled as Zach pulled Dusty out of the small alcove.

"I suppose you don't wear a helmet, either."

"Sometimes, when it's a new bull, but I prefer not to. I think the animal knows if I'm trying to protect myself from him."

Zach shook his head. This woman was a handful. "Chaps?"

"I have them."

"Glove?"

"A Tiffany glove. A gift from Papa before he died."

"Vest?"

"Of course. I'm not a complete half-wit."

"Mouth guard?"

She shook her head. "I don't like the way it feels in the back of my mouth. Makes me want to gag."

"Jesus." Zach raked his fingers through his hair. "I'm going to insist on the spurs, darlin'. Not that you'll need 'em, cause you're not gonna ride Diablo anyway."

"But I suppose if I do convince you, I have to have the spurs."

"You got it."

"I don't want to spend so much money."

"I told you, my treat."

"I can't let you do that. We barely know each other."

"Heck, we've known each other for twenty-plus years. I've got body hair I haven't known as long."

Dusty's laugh rang out like jingling bells.

"Now there's a cheery sound. Let me buy you the gift, darlin'."

"You just bought me dinner."

"Okay, it'll be a gift in memory of our dinner."

She sighed. He could tell she wanted to accept, but something was stopping her.

"You don't owe me anything. It's just a gift."

"Oh, I didn't think..." She turned an adorable shade of red.

"I know you didn't." He walked back into the spur shop and spoke to Jay. "Let's set her up."

"Will do."

Fifteen minutes later, Jay was wrapping up a new set of bull riding spurs for Dusty.

"You don't have to get the straps, Zach," Dusty said, clearly embarrassed when Jay indicated the price was $93.95 for the whole spur package. "I can use my old ones. That'll take the cost down a little."

"If you want to ride my bull, darlin', you need the best," Zach said. "Straps, shanks, rowels, and all. Brand spankin' new and made for bull riding." Although he still had no intention of letting her ride Diablo, he hoped the comment would ease her obvious discomfort with the expense.

Jay sat down to write out the invoice. "You'll have to pardon me," he said. "My register broke down so I'm figuring tax by hand." He scribbled hastily.

"What's the tax rate here?" Dusty asked.

"Eight point one-two-five percent."

"So tax on ninety-three ninety-five would be seven sixty-three."

"Damn," Jay said, shaking his head. "Don't have a clue if she's right, but we'll go with it."

"I'm right."

"Amazing, darlin'," Zach said. "How'd you do that?"

"I told you I was good at math."

"There's good and there's genius. Go figure." He took the package from Jay, and they walked out of the shop. "If I'd known you could do that, I'd have asked you to figure the tip at dinner."

"I'd've been glad to." She shyly put her hand in his. "Thank you for the gift," she said. "I should get something for you."

"Don't need anything."

"You said you needed a new hat."

"Changed my mind." She didn't have the money to buy the kind of hat he wanted.

"You have to let me do something."

"How about a cold drink?"

"That's hardly payment for those." She motioned to the package in Zach's hand.

"A hot drink?"

She gave him a friendly punch in the arm. "You're incorrigible."

"'Fraid so, darlin'."

He took her hand, and they walked around the pavilion.

Dusty's eyes were wide as she looked at the displays of ostrich boots. Zach opened his mouth to offer to buy her some and then thought better of it. She was right. They barely knew each other. So why did he want to buy her everything she touched? Everything that made her eyes light up like the night sky in the country? A strange feeling, but a pleasant one.

When the vendors started packing up their wares for the evening, Zach guided Dusty out to the parking lot to the Jaguar. They drove to her hotel, laughing together. When he walked her to her room, they stood for an awkward moment. Dusty thanked him for the dinner and the spurs, and they made plans to meet in the morning to work with Diablo.

"But don't get your hopes up, darlin'," Zach said, winking at her. "I still ain't gonna let you ride him."

Dusty stomped her foot perilously close to Zach's expensively shod toe. Clearly, he'd hit a nerve. Again.

"I told you, I'm not your darling. And why do you say *ain't* all the time? You went to Harvard, for God's sake!"

Zach arched his eyebrows and grinned. "Now you sound like my mama. I've been talkin' this way my whole life, and I *ain't* gonna stop now, *darlin'*."

Dusty exhaled sharply as she fished in her purse, presumably for her key card. She looked up at Zach. "Don't let me keep you. I'll be fine."

"I can't go yet." His heart slammed against his sternum as he placed his palms on the wall, trapping her. "There's something I need to do first."

"What?"

Her chocolate eyes widened, and he swore he could see her soul.

"This."

He crushed his lips down on hers.

CHAPTER THREE

Infuriating. Sexist Pig. Idiot genius who didn't care about proper English usage.

But oh, could the man kiss.

From the first second, refusing wasn't an option. The unimaginable sensation of his mouth pressed to hers overrode the rational part of Dusty's brain. His lips were warm, unexpectedly soft, and laced with the robust boldness of his after-dinner Irish coffee. The bewitching friction as he nibbled at her mouth enticed her lips to open.

And then—magic. The woodsy spiciness of the coffee, the tangy storm of the Irish whiskey, and something else... something unique and indescribable. Zach. His tongue danced around hers, and her legs trembled beneath her. As if on cue, he wrapped one strong arm around her waist and pulled her to him. Every cell in her body screamed at her to drive into him, to deepen the kiss, but she was frightened. She barely knew him. So she began to pull away.

His strength defeated hers. "Kiss me back, darlin'," he whispered against her chin. "Please."

The *please* did it. Somehow, she knew instinctively that Zach McCray didn't utter that word very often, if at all. Weak-kneed and aroused, she thrust her tongue into the moist warmth of his mouth, and she was lost.

She'd done her share of kissing in the past, but never had she felt such an adventurous surge of need and desire. The frantic necking in parked cars, the careless good night kisses, the lazy exploration—nothing compared to this urgency, this demand. As their tongues tangled together, she moved her hands upward, framing his face. She toyed with the roughness of his night beard, the sleekness of his jawline. Part of her was barely cognizant of him cupping her cheeks, his thumbs caressing her, yet another part was hyper-aware of his touch, his mastery of her.

When the frenzy between them slackened slightly, he removed his lips from hers and trailed them across her cheek, down her neck, and to her ear, tracing it with his tongue, nipping the soft lobe. She kissed his neck and inhaled his scent. Cloves. And pine. The outdoors. Heavenly. Faint moans met her ears, and she realized they were coming from her throat.

"Dusty." Zach's voice was husky, smoke-filled.

She moaned again as his mouth found hers. Unrestrained desire took her over, and she thrust her hips against him, feeling the strength of his arousal. She imagined him inside her, filling her, pleasuring her with that gorgeous body. She had never wanted a man like this. She wanted him naked, on top of her, doing things no man had ever done to her.

She let out a disappointed rasp as he broke the kiss and headed for her ear again.

"God, you're beautiful," he whispered. "Let's go inside."

"Oh yes, yes." Dusty tunneled her fingers through his silky hair, leading him back to her mouth.

He pushed his tongue into her again and retreated. "Now, darlin'. Or I take you right here."

"Yes, yes." Then, "Oh! I mean no. No!" She placed her palms on his chest—oh, how she wanted him to lose the shirt—and pushed.

"What's the matter?" He fingered a stray curl that had come loose from her braid.

"I...that is, you...can't come in."

"Please."

That word again. But, "No. I—I...my brother might be there. We're sharing this room."

He backed away from her, a look of surprise on his face. But it softened almost instantly. "I'll take you to my hotel."

Oh, those eyes. They penetrated her with a fiery passion that started her pulse racing again. But Dusty shook her head. "Sam would worry."

Besides, this insanity would no doubt calm itself during the drive, and they would both regain their composure. They'd get to his room and the magic would be gone. What was done was done. She had enjoyed it, but it was over.

"Leave him a note." He leaned in and brushed his lips across hers.

Such a sweet, tender gesture, but the gentle force of it landed between her legs like a torpedo. Okay, so maybe the insanity wouldn't calm itself *quite* yet.

"I can't. I'm sorry." Her hands shook as she fumbled in her purse and drew out the key card. Quickly, without looking at him, she slid it into the lock and let herself in, closing the door behind her. She stood alone, leaning against the door, her heart thumping wildly, the heat between her legs aching. Closing her eyes, she felt him on the other side of the door, the hot energy of his body suffusing the barrier between them, reaching out to her. She willed her body to steady itself.

A one-night stand with Zach McCray was the last thing she needed.

★ ★ ★

Zach's body slumped against the door to Dusty's hotel room, the unsated hunger of his arousal a dead weight in his jeans. Frustrated, he pounded on the door.

"Dusty. Darlin'. Let me in. *Please.*"

If she heard him, she made no indication. She must have gone in to take a shower or something. Funny, he could have sworn he felt her presence through the door.

"Damn," he said aloud.

He could still taste the sweet honey of her mouth, smell the fresh spring scent of her. Her lips had parted for him with such innocent ardor, but then she had kissed him like a temptress, a siren. Like no one had ever kissed him before. He groaned. He wanted to break that damn door down, toss her on the bed, and pound into her, making her his.

But no, he couldn't. He walked, in pain, to the elevator and made his way to the lobby and then to his rental car.

And back to the hotel for a cold shower.

★ ★ ★

For about thirty seconds the next morning, Dusty considered standing Zach up. But she was a polite western girl, and they had made plans to meet and work with Diablo. She really wanted to ride that bull. And, she finally admitted to herself, she wanted to see Zach.

She had no intention of kissing him again. That was a complication she didn't want in her life right now. No, her interest in Zach McCray was purely bovine in nature. She'd make sure of it.

He was waiting for her by Diablo's pen, looking sexy

as hell in worn Wranglers and a light blue western shirt that matched his left eye. He'd left the expensive ostrich footwear at the hotel. Today he wore a pair of worn brown leather cowboy boots.

"Mornin', darlin'." He tipped his Stetson.

"Good morning, yourself," she said, purposefully avoiding his gaze. She set down the tote bag that held her chaps, vest, glove, and brand new spurs. "Diablo looks pretty mellow today." She cased the bull's pen, noting his stance, his attitude.

"He's always mellow in the morning. That's why I suggested we meet at this time." Zach walked over to her and touched her elbow.

How could such an innocent contact make her whole body sizzle? She slowly exhaled and moved away from him.

"Why don't you tell me what you plan to do?"

"I kind of play it by ear."

"I see." He took off his hat and set it on a fence post. "So tell me how you'll play it by ear. What's your philosophy?"

Dusty stood her ground. "The most important thing is not to fear the bull. He can sense fear. All animals can."

"But darlin', this here's a big ass bull. Fear is okay."

"No, it's not. He'll know if I'm afraid of him. And I'm not afraid of him."

"How can you not be?"

"Because I'm not. There are worse things in life than a big bull. Many other things that are worthy of my fear. But not Diablo."

"You're something else." Zach chuckled. "I don't know any other woman who wouldn't be afraid of this brute."

"There's no reason to be. He doesn't want to hurt me."

"How can you conquer him with that attitude?"

"You're such a man. You men always want to conquer. I have no desire to conquer Diablo. I want to befriend him."

"Oh, God."

"I don't want to be his master. If we're equals, we'll understand each other. He'll want to help me."

"But you'll still be breaking him."

"No. No, I won't. I don't see it that way."

"We're talking semantics here, darlin'."

Dusty thought for a moment. "Maybe," she admitted, "but it's all in the attitude, Zach. He'd know if I were trying to break him, and he'd fight back. So I'll befriend him. I'll give him what he wants."

"What is it that he wants, darlin'?" Zach smiled lazily. "Other than a cow in season."

"Ha-ha." Dusty rolled her eyes. "He wants what any living creature wants. Respect. Understanding." She swallowed hard. "Love."

"Love, huh?" Zach winked at her.

"Oh, don't look at me like I have two heads. All creatures want love. And if I give it to him, he won't hurt me. He won't want to."

"He might."

"No, he won't. He doesn't want to hurt me. I can tell just by looking at him."

"How so?"

"His eyes. He and I understand each other."

"Okay. I guess I'll accept that answer."

"It's the only one you're going to get."

"Fine. Tell me now, what else do you do to prepare?"

"I keep myself physically fit, obviously."

"Oh, yeah." He eyed her up and down. "Obviously."

"And I visualize. From the time I start preparations in the chute to the time I'm done with the ride, I'm visualizing every possible move and countermove he might make. I see myself as a winner."

"You have a lot of confidence."

"Not really. I just don't accept loss as an option."

"But loss is a fact of life, darlin'."

"Sure it is. But you can't go into something with that attitude, Zach. You're a bull rider yourself. You must know that."

"Sure, but—"

"Plus, seeing myself as a winner is the best fear controller there is. So it helps in that respect, too."

"Okay." Zach touched her shoulder. "Your philosophy on bull riding is a little idiosyncratic, but I like it. What do you want to do first?"

"I'd like to talk to him a little. My voice seems to have a soothing effect on animals, bulls in particular. At least, it has in the past."

"Talk away."

He smiled. The man had a beautiful set of teeth—no doubt the best orthodontia Jason McCray had been able to buy—framed by those incredible and talented lips.

"Just don't expect him to answer."

"Funny." Dusty closed her eyes, mentally releasing all fear and stress from her body. Such a mental wipe was imperative if she wanted the animal to trust her. She breathed deeply, settled herself in her happy place—her grassy meadow at her Montana ranch. After a few minutes, she opened her eyes, walked to the front of Diablo's pen, made eye contact, and began crooning in the sing-song voice that had met with success in the past. She told the bull what a big strong boy he was, how she wasn't going to hurt him, to please let her in. Soon, Diablo was her whole universe. Nothing else existed. She began to sing softly to him, the lullaby her mama used to sing to her years and years ago, before she got sick.

Over in Killarney
Many years ago,
Me mother sang a song to me
In tones so sweet and low.
Just a simple little ditty,
In her good ould Irish way,
And I'd give the world if she could sing
That song to me this day.
Toora loora looral, Toora loora li,
Toora loora looral, hush now, don't you cry.
Toora loora looral, Toora loora li,
Toora loora looral, that's an Irish lullaby.
Oft in dreams I wander
To that cot again,
I feel her arms a-huggin' me
As when she held me then.
And I hear her voice a-hummin'
To me as in days of yore,
When she used to rock me fast asleep
Outside the cabin door.
Toora loora looral, Toora loora li,
Toora loora looral, hush now, don't you cry.
Toora loora looral, Toora loora li,
Toora loora looral, that's an Irish lullaby.

With tears misting in her eyes, Dusty reached out and touched Diablo's cheek.

"No!" Zach rushed toward her, tackling her to the ground to get her away from the bull. "He doesn't like to be touched on his face!"

"Damn it, Zach!" Dusty sat up and brushed the dirt from her jeans. "I was making great progress. He wasn't going to hurt me. He's penned up!"

"I couldn't take the chance." Zach rubbed her cheek. "Just a little dust," he said, catching a tear with his finger. He held it out to show her and then touched it to his lips. "That song was the prettiest thing I've ever heard."

"For all the good you let it do." She sniffed and willed the threatening tears not to fall.

"I've never heard it before."

"Please. Of course you have. You're Irish, aren't you?"

"McCray is a Scottish name, and my ma's of English descent."

"Oh. Well, my mama used to sing it to me." Dusty sighed. "A long, long time ago..."

"And now you sing it to bulls." He smiled, his eyes kind as he touched her cheek again.

She tried to ignore the tingle he aroused in her. "Who else is there to sing it to? Besides, it works. You saw Diablo respond. If you hadn't interfered—"

"I was thinking of the words of the song. It says you'd give the world if she could sing it to you again. That's why it made you cry, isn't it?"

"I'm not crying."

But a lone tear chose that exact moment to fall. Zach smiled as he caught it again. "Of course not."

"Look, we're wasting time here. I've got to start over with Diablo now." Dusty brushed off her legs again and began to rise.

Zach got to his feet first and held out his hand. Although warmth flooded her cheeks, she took it. He pulled her to him and kissed her gently on the cheek.

"I was always so sorry about what happened to your mama. How she got sick and all."

"It's all right. I don't remember much. I was young."

"You remember more than you think you do. You remember that song."

Dusty said nothing as Zach lifted her chin so she was looking straight into his eyes. "You were such a cute little tomboy back then. I knew you didn't understand what was happening to your mama. I always wished I could make it better for you."

Dusty widened her eyes. "Did you? You always picked on me."

"That was just me being an idiot kid," Zach said. "When I found out your mama was terminal and they couldn't help her anymore, I wished I had the power of God to erase that sadness in your big brown eyes." He skimmed his callused thumb over her lips.

Words, mere words, but they touched her even more than the spark of his fingers on her mouth. "That's kind of you. I had no idea."

"I know you didn't."

"Well..." Dusty struggled to regain her composure. "We survived."

"But you still miss her."

"I probably always will. Don't you miss your father?"

"Yeah, I do. But I was a grown man when he died. It's different."

"I suppose so. It was different when my papa died."

"Hey"—he cupped her cheek in his hand—"do you want to take a break? I haven't had breakfast yet. I'm famished, and I could use some caffeine."

"But Diablo—"

"I'll bring you back here after we eat," he said.

"And you'll try not to interfere?"

He grinned broadly. "Can't make that promise, darlin'."

Dusty shrugged her shoulders. A girl had to eat. "Fine. I'm hungry anyway."

★ ★ ★

Again, Zach relished watching Dusty eat. He wondered for a moment how she could stay so fit when she ate like a horse, but then realized she stayed lean the same way he did. Ranch work and rodeos. When his stomach was full and two cups of coffee had given him the burst he needed, he brought Dusty back to Diablo's pen.

"All right," she said, looking at him fiercely. "I'm going to try again now. *No interfering.*"

"You going to sing that pretty song again?"

"Eventually. You don't stop doing what works. How about you stand over there?" She pointed to a couple bales of hay next to one of the practice rings.

"Sorry, darlin.' I stay here. That was the deal."

"Zach, please?"

"Look"—he cupped her face in both hands—"I need to be serious for a minute. I know you think you can handle this bull, but up until now, I'm the only one who he's even halfway listened to. I need to be here. I can't risk you getting hurt."

"I never knew you cared." She smiled.

Was she flirting? He looked into her big baby browns. No, definitely not flirting. Facetiousness, that's what it was. The fact was he *did* care. He cared about anyone who might get injured by his livestock. "Of course I care. Diablo's my responsibility, and so is anyone who comes in contact with him."

"Then why did you offer the purse to anyone who could ride him? Surely you know it's possible that someone could get hurt."

"That's what disclaimers are for, darlin'."

"Do you want me to sign your disclaimer? I'd be happy to, because I can tell you right now that this bull is not going to hurt me."

He shook his head. She was something else. Her steadfast obstinacy only made her more appealing. She continued to stare at him indignantly. Her long braid had fallen over one shoulder, curving over the knoll of her chest. He imagined her hair unbraided, a mass of golden curls flowing around her naked breasts, hardened ruby nipples peeking through.

God, I have to get a grip. I don't need a boner right now.

"I don't want you to sign anything. I won't let him hurt you."

Dusty nodded and turned to Diablo.

As she walked around the pen and spoke softly, a shrill noise cut into his thoughts.

"Zach! There you are!"

Dusty turned toward the commotion, her eyebrows raised. "Who's that?"

He didn't have to turn around. He recognized the voice.

Angelina. His ex-fiancée.

CHAPTER FOUR

Zach didn't answer. The tall slender woman approached Diablo's pen. Her brown curls were pulled into two bunches over each ear, and she wore crisp jeans and a pink gingham blouse. Dusty groaned. Who did she think she was? Mary Ann from *Gilligan's Island*?

The woman threw her arms around Zach and kissed his cheek. "How are you? I've been hoping to run into you."

"I'm fine."

"And who might this be?" she asked, looking behind Zach at Dusty, who stood next to Diablo's pen. The bull munched hungrily at some hay.

"Oh. This is Dusty. Dusty O'Donovan. Her pa used to work at McCray Landing."

"Silly"—the woman tossed her twin ponytails, her hands on Zach's shoulders—"I didn't mean *her*. I meant the bull."

Mary Ann's giggling laughter grated. Yeah, funny. She meant the bull. Dusty walked toward them. She wouldn't be ignored or belittled.

"The bull's Diablo," she said. "And I'm going to ride him."

Zach cleared his throat. "Darlin', I've told you before—"

"And you are?" Dusty interrupted, holding out her hand.

The woman shook Dusty's hand limply. "Angelina," she said. "Angelina Bay. Zach and I are...that is, we *used* to be engaged."

"Nice to meet you, Angelina," Dusty said sweetly. "Are

you involved in the rodeo?"

"Oh, goodness no." She tossed her ponytails again. "My brother is though. He's a bronc buster and a bull rider. And my daddy's entering some livestock in the show. We raise prime beef at our ranch. I'm sure you've heard of it, Bay Crossing? On the western slope?"

"Can't say that I have," Dusty said, rubbing her hands on her thighs. Her palms were sweaty for some reason.

"Dusty's from Montana," Zach said.

"How nice. Do you ride bulls there, Donna?"

While Dusty seethed, Zach answered for her. "It's Dusty."

"Of course, what a cute little name."

"Isn't it?" Dusty fought her anger, wishing she could control the crimson she knew was rising in her cheeks. "And yes, I do ride bulls in Montana. And here."

"A female bull rider. You must be tough as nails."

"It's not toughness that makes a good bull rider, Andromeda."

"It's Angelina."

"Of course." Dusty smirked. Resisting the urge to add the *"what a cute little name"* remark showed her maturity. Okay, even *she* didn't buy that, but Andromeda had been a good one. Inspired.

"If you'll excuse us, Angie," Zach said, "Dusty and I have some work to do with Diablo."

"So this is the one with the half mil purse," Angelina said, ignoring Zach's obvious attempt to get rid of her.

"Yes," Dusty said, before Zach could open his mouth to respond.

"I bet Harper could ride him," Angelina said.

"Who's Harper?" Dusty asked.

"My brother. He's a champ."

"He's welcome to try," Zach said, "as long as he signs the disclaimer. You remember Chad's accident last year, don't you?"

"Yes. But honestly, Zach, I think Harper's a better rider than Chad."

Zach snorted. "I beg to differ, but he can try if he wants to."

"I'll definitely speak to him about it," she said. Then, "I'd love to get together for lunch and catch up. Are you free today?"

"'Fraid not."

"Oh, shoot." Angelina's lips turned into a pout. "How about tonight then? Harper and I are throwing a gala in the Westminster room at the Windsor. You've got to come."

"Dusty and I have plans."

"We do?"

"Yeah, darlin', we do," Zach said, winking at her.

"Shucks," Angelina said, batting her eyes. "You two make a cute little couple."

"Oh, we're not a cou—"

"Hush, darlin'." Zach's arms went around Dusty and he pulled her close.

"Please say you'll come, Zach. You can bring her along."

Zach cleared his throat. "We appreciate the invitation, Angie, but—"

"We'd love to come," Dusty said, interrupting. "We absolutely wouldn't miss it. What time?"

"Around eight. Heavy appetizers and desserts. And an open bar, of course."

"You don't mind if we invite Chad along do you? And my brother? He and Chad are old friends."

"Of course." Angelina's lips broadened in a saccharine

smile. "We'd love to have them." She turned to focus on Zach. "I ran into Chelsea earlier and invited her and Dallas. I'm looking forward to seeing all of you. Ta-ta." Angelina turned to walk away, but looked over her shoulder. "I'll have Harper get in touch with you about the bull."

"You do that," Zach said, sliding his hand down Dusty's back to squeeze the cheek of her bottom.

Dusty jolted. "What the hell are you doing?" Her whisper was urgent. "She can't even see that."

"So? You deserve it for telling her we'd go to her shindig."

Dusty shrugged away from him. "Serves you right, for trying to use me as a pawn in your love life."

"Now, darlin'"—he pulled her into his embrace again—"I have no intention of using you as a pawn. But I do want you in my love life."

When his mouth came down on hers, Dusty gasped, giving him the opening he sought.

Oh God, oh God, oh God. Magic again. His mouth was as silky and sweet as it had been the night before, and his tongue was just as carnal and relentless. The kiss was unwavering, drugging. Dusty responded. She had no choice. She moaned as she surrendered.

When he withdrew his tongue, she whimpered at the loss, but when he started nibbling his way across her bottom lip, she shuddered. When he sucked it between his teeth, she hissed. And when he licked inside her lips, running his tongue around her teeth and gums in little flicks, her knees weakened and she nearly swooned.

He caught her in his strong arms. "That's right, darlin'. Just enjoy it." He continued his assault on her mouth.

Oh, the sensation, the sweet joining of tongues. Dusty gave in to his domination of her mouth. She wilted in his arms as he licked and bit at her. He not only gave, he took, kissing her with a reckless abandon she had never known. She was losing herself, but she didn't care.

A soft smack echoed as Zach broke the kiss. Dusty gasped, panting and puffing as he nibbled on her neck, her ear.

"Come with me, darlin'," he whispered, and took her hand and walked briskly toward a blue pickup.

Dusty tried to break free, but he held her firmly.

"Oh, no, you're not getting away from me this time."

They reached the truck, and he grabbed her and kissed her again, completely eradicating her will to refuse him.

Her eyes closed and her mind reeling, she felt him open the door of the truck behind her and gently shove her inside. Before she had time to think, he was beside her in the driver's seat and had pulled her into his arms again. He pressed his lips to her neck as he fumbled with the buttons on her shirt, pulling the tail from her waistband. Soon his big strong hands were on her breasts, kneading them, thumbing her erect nipples through her lacy bra.

"Oh, God," he murmured. "You're so perfect. So beautiful." He lowered his head and took a rosy nipple in his mouth, sucking her through the fabric.

Her muscles tightened as desire rushed through her. She was a goner now. But at twenty-three, she wasn't going to have sex in a car like some horny teenager.

"Zach." She hardly recognized her own voice.

"What, darlin'?" He panted in her ear.

"I...I'm not going to screw you in a truck." She trembled as he pushed her bra up, releasing her breasts to fall gently against her chest.

"We're not going to screw." He kissed the plump white skin surrounding her nipple and flicked his tongue over the rosy bud.

Dusty jolted backward, but his arm steadied her.

"We're going to make slow, sweet, passionate love."

Oh God, yes. Slow, sweet, passionate love. But not in a truck.

"But not in your truck, Zach."

"No," he rasped, "not in a truck." He tongued her nipple, biting it gently and tugging.

She squirmed against the dampness between her legs. He sucked one nipple and then the other, using his teeth, his lips, and his tongue to torment her. She heard herself moaning, whispering words of encouragement for him to keep going. What was happening to her?

Her nipples were deep scarlet and tingling when he cupped her breasts gently and returned to her mouth for another firm kiss.

"I want you so much," he said into her mouth. "I want to make love to you."

"Yes, Zach." She puffed against his cheek. "Yes, make love to me."

"I want you naked, under me."

"Oh, yes."

"I want to sink myself deep inside you."

"God, yes. Yes."

He grabbed her hand and led it to his arousal. Dusty reveled at the hardness under her palm. She began to stimulate him through his jeans.

"Oh, yeah, darlin'. That feels so good."

He slid her shirt from her shoulder and kissed her there,

bit into her, and licked to soothe the sting.

"Zach." Her voice sounded husky, throaty.

"Hmm?" He slid his tongue over her shoulder, up her neck, nuzzling her pulse point.

"Not here."

"Right." He broke away from her, leaning back in his seat, beads of sweat trickling from his brow. Her hand was still on his crotch. "Damn." He exhaled slowly, his breath whooshing from his strong body. "You get to me, woman."

Dusty removed her hand from him and leaned back into the passenger seat, trying to steady her breathing. "I-I don't mean to."

He reached for her hand and entwined their fingers together. "It's not a bad thing, darlin'."

With those words, she catapulted back into reality. It *was* a bad thing. She had to stop it.

Oh, she didn't want to. She ached for him, for his kisses, for his touch, for his sex embedded deep inside her. But she had to end this. She couldn't get close to him, couldn't let him in.

Couldn't risk him learning the truth.

Quick as lightning, she disentangled her hand from his, grabbed the door handle, and fled.

CHAPTER FIVE

Zach cursed as Dusty ran away from him, her shirttail billowing in the winter breeze. The Colorado winter was mild, an Indian summer that had continued through January. No snow to speak of yet. Zach wanted to run after her, to find out what was wrong, but he was so hard he couldn't move.

What was it about this woman? He wanted her like he had never wanted anything. Clearly, she felt it too. So why did she keep running away?

He fished his keys out of his pocket, turned on the engine of his truck, and opened the windows, letting the January breeze flow through the cab. He thought it might help him cool off, but he didn't hold much hope. He wanted to go after her, but she was out of sight now, and he had no idea where to look.

What could be troubling her? Was it his fault? He was the one who'd forced her to talk about her mother earlier, but she had seemed okay with that. Maybe it was the money thing. She and Sam were sharing a hotel room. Were things really that tight for them? Only one person, besides Dusty, had the answers. He grabbed his cell phone and dialed Chad.

"Hey, Zach," Chad said into his ear.

"Hey. Have you seen Sam this morning?"

"Yeah, he's right here with me. We're checking out some of the livestock, and then we're going to head out for a bite of lunch. You want to meet us?"

"That'd be great, little brother."

"Hey, I'm taller than you are."

"You're still my little brother. Where should I meet you?"

"M and D's Barbecue. In about half an hour."

"Great. I'll be there."

And I will find out what is going on with Dusty. Figuring out that sweet little thing had somehow become a priority for him.

★ ★ ★

M and D's had the best barbecue in the nation. At least in Chad's vocal opinion, and Zach agreed. Sam, however, had tears in his eyes and water running out his nose after the first few bites.

"I told you not to get the spicy sauce," Chad said, laughing at his friend. "A Montana boy can't take all the pequin and jalapenos."

"Peking what?" Sam said, reaching for his water glass.

"Not Peking, you moron. This ain't China. Pe-*keen*. As in hot chile peppers." Chad motioned to their waitress. "We're gonna need lots more water here. And a few Kleenex, please." Chad turned to his brother. "You're quiet today."

"Ain't much to say." Zach munched on his ribs and turned to Sam. "O'Donovan, you're red as a beet."

"Really, I'm fine." Sam coughed and drank more water.

"Dusty and I worked with Diablo this morning," Zach heard himself say.

"Yeah?" Sam wiped his hands on his napkin. "How'd she do?"

"Okay, I guess. She sang him a lullaby."

Chad erupted in laughter. "You're kidding."

"He's not kidding," Sam said. "It's an old Irish lullaby our mama used to sing. It seems to work on bulls. At least it works for her."

Chad rolled his eyes. "Whatever you say."

Zach continued. "She did well with him actually. He seemed to respond. Truthfully, I was the one who got a little nervous. She reached out to touch him, and I freaked."

"Dusty has good instincts," Sam said. "You don't have to worry about her with the bull. After all, he's in a pen, and she's not stupid."

"I know she's not. She's not afraid, either."

"Nope. There's not much that scares Dusty."

"Why is that?"

Sam fidgeted, but said nothing. Zach sensed a story there, but Sam wasn't going to offer it.

"She seems intelligent, too. She did an amazing calculation in her head yesterday," Zach said.

"Yeah, she's a whiz with numbers," Sam said.

Zach touched his napkin to his lips. "Tell me, why didn't she finish college?"

"She told you about that?"

"Yeah, she said she only went for a year. Was it money?"

Sam cleared his throat. "I think it's best if you ask her about that. It's not my story to tell."

"Are there problems at your ranch?" Zach asked.

"Nothing we can't handle."

"Look, I care about your sister. I only want to help her."

"Care about her? You hadn't seen her in seventeen years until yesterday."

"I...like her."

"Aw, geez," Sam said. "Not you too."

"What do you mean by that? She said she didn't have a boyfriend."

"She doesn't."

"Then what's the problem?"

"I'm just tired of chasing away her potential suitors, that's all."

"You mean there's a lot of them?" A wave of possessive jealousy punched Zach's gut.

"More than you can imagine. My baby sister's a regular stud magnet. And she's usually not interested, so I'm the one who has to get rid of the persistent ones."

A thrill tingled through Zach. So she wasn't interested in most of them, but she definitely seemed interested in him. Then again, she had run away from him twice now.

"Why isn't she interested? Are they all losers or something?"

"Nah. She's just..." Sam stopped. "Look, you really need to ask Dusty these questions, man. I'm not comfortable with this."

"Fair enough." Zach stopped pushing. He would ask Dusty. Tonight. "By the way, Dusty and I ran into Angie this morning. She invited us all to some shindig tonight in the Westminster Room at our hotel. Dallas and Chelsea are going."

"Hang out with our self-important older brother and his prima donna wife? Count me out. Besides, Sam and I were going to cruise the bars."

"Look, I don't want to hang out with Dallas any more than you do, but cruising the bars? Grow up, will you?"

"And stop having fun? I'm not that old, bro."

"Then put off your cruising until tomorrow. Dusty and I need the two of you to go to the Bay thing tonight."

"Aw, Zach. Name one reason why we should go hang out with Angelina Bay. And Chelsea. God."

"Free beer?"

Chad smiled. "Now that's one good reason, brother."

★ ★ ★

The Westminster Room at the Windsor Hotel could have doubled for the Queen's parlor at Buckingham Palace. At least that's how it seemed to Dusty. The Bays were apparently as rich, or richer, than the McCrays. Dusty felt underdressed in her black skirt and creamy silk blouse, though Zach had assured her she looked gorgeous. Most of the women wore cocktail attire. Not that Dusty had any cocktail attire.

Zach looked luscious in black trousers and a white oxford, no tie. A smattering of ebony chest hair peeked out from his collar. Sexy. Sam and Chad had already arrived and were hanging out at the bar, having engaged a few available women. Dusty shook her head.

"Your brother's a bad influence on my brother."

"Darlin', my brother's a bad influence on everyone. But I think Sam can take care of himself."

"If you say so. It seems the two of them are cut from the same cloth."

"Both about six-four, good looking, what do you expect?"

"I expect my brother to act his age."

"Yeah, well, good luck with that."

Dusty sighed. "Now what?"

"We pay respects to our hostess, I guess."

"You can't wait to see her, can you?"

"Now just a minute—"

"Cool off. I'm just joking." Dusty smiled at him. "I can charm the pants off anyone. Just look how I fared with Diablo."

"Darlin', I don't doubt it for a minute. Come on."

Zach grabbed her hand and led her to Angelina, who was talking to a tall, nice looking man. Angelina looked quite pretty, much to Dusty's dismay, in a dark plum satin dress that fell below her knees, accented by strappy black sandals. Dusty felt frumpy in her skirt and blouse and black pumps. Angelina's hair had been let loose from the Mary Ann bunches and fell in dark waves to her shoulders.

At least my hair is just as nice as hers, Dusty thought, *and longer.* She shook her head, the red-blond waves falling midway down her back.

"Zach!" Angelina gushed, leaving the dark-haired man. "I'm so glad you came. And Donna. It's nice to see you again."

"Dusty," Zach said, his lips pursed. "Thank you for having us."

"Make yourselves at home. We have plenty of food and drink. The deejay'll be firing up in a half hour or so. I hope you'll save me a dance."

"Sure." Zach cleared his throat. "Come on, darlin'," he said to Dusty. "Let's get a drink." He led her to the bar.

"What would you like?" Zach asked her.

"A glass of Merlot sounds nice," Dusty said.

"Merlot for the lady," Zach said, "and Wild Turkey neat for me." Zach placed a ten dollar bill in the tip jar.

"I changed my mind," Dusty said to the bartender. "I'll have what he's having." What the hell? She needed a little something wild to get her through this evening. There was Mary Ann to deal with. And Zach was eventually going to ask her why she had run that afternoon. She was surprised he hadn't brought it up yet.

"You want to sit down?" he asked.

"Let's go see what Chad and Sam are up to." She gestured to a table where the two men were chatting with two young women.

"Darlin', we'd be third wheels."

"Come on." She pulled on his arm. "They're our brothers."

"So?"

"I'm sure they're dying to talk to us."

"Doesn't look that way to me."

She led him to the table anyway. "Hey, Sam, Chad."

"Hey, Dust." Sam turned to his companions. "This is my baby sister, Dusty. Dusty, meet Sydney Buchanan and Linda Rhine."

"And this is my big brother, Zach," Chad said. "You all want to sit down?"

"We'd love to," Dusty cooed.

"Sydney's a barrel racer," Sam said. "I've been telling her all about you."

"Are you competing?" Dusty asked.

"Yeah. Day after tomorrow. You?"

"Day after tomorrow. Good luck to you."

"You, too. Though I doubt you'll need it. Sam told me about your best time. Thirteen point nine seconds is awesome."

"Sydney's real good, too," Sam said. "Her personal best is fourteen point one."

"That's exceptional," Dusty said. "I see you'll be some real competition."

"You want to dance, darlin'?" Zach asked her. "They're firing up the music."

"Sure." Dusty shivered as Zach took her hand and led her

to the small dance floor. "I didn't know you danced."

"I don't. But I wanted to get away from that table."

"Why?"

"Because I want to hang out with you."

"So we're not going to dance then?"

"Depends on what they play. In fact, excuse me for a minute."

Dusty watched as Zach approached the deejay, whispered to him, and handed him a folded bill. As he walked back toward Dusty, the harmonious voices of Tim McGraw and Faith Hill began to sing "Like We Never Loved at All."

"This is our dance, darlin'," he said, taking her into his arms.

He didn't try to hold her in the traditional dance pose. Both of his arms went around her body and pulled her close. She had no choice but to wrap her arms around his neck. As her body met his, she melted into him. Soft cotton shirt. Warm hard man. So good.

"Mmm," she heard herself say.

"What's that?" he whispered.

"Nothing. It's just...this feels so nice."

"Sure does."

He pulled her even closer, and she snuggled her cheek against his shoulder, breathing in his crisp masculine scent.

"Have I told you how beautiful you look tonight?" he whispered.

She chuckled softly. "Yes."

"Have I told you how much I want to kiss you?"

"No."

"In that case. I really want to kiss you. I can't think of anything else when I look at those sweet lips of yours."

Dusty's skin tingled. She sighed into his chest, her nose nuzzling the exposed black hair. Without thinking, she brushed her lips against it.

"That's nice, darlin'." He reciprocated by leaning down and pressing his mouth to her neck.

She shuddered.

"You want to go up to my room?" he asked.

Her heart beat so hard against her chest, she was certain he could feel it. "Can't we get something to eat?"

"Sure. If you want to."

When the song ended, he took her to the buffet line and they filled their plates with prawns, oysters, bruschetta, and myriad other goodies. They replenished their drinks and sat down at an empty table.

"Great spread," Dusty said.

"Angie never does anything halfway," Zach replied, munching on a chicken wing.

"It was nice of her to invite us."

"I suppose so. I'd rather be at a quiet dinner with you."

Her cheeks warmed. "You make me feel all..."

"All what?" The corners of his mouth crinkled. God, his smile was something out of heaven itself.

"All...I don't know...mushy inside."

"Good."

He sucked an oyster off its shell, and the slurping sound made Dusty want to grab him and kiss him senseless.

"Tell me something, darlin'. Why do you keep running from me?"

"It's complicated—" she began, but thankfully was interrupted by Sam and Chad, accompanied by Sydney and the other girl. Dusty couldn't remember her name. Lori? Lila?

She had to stop drinking Wild Turkey.

"We're heading out," Chad said. "We're going for a late supper at Amici's. You all want to come?"

Dusty started to answer, but Zach beat her to it. "No, thanks. We have plans."

"We do?" Dusty said after they'd left.

"Sure we do. Don't we?" He winked at her.

"Could you excuse me for a few minutes? I need to use the ladies room." Dusty scurried away, trying to ignore Zach's bewildered look. When she reached the restroom, she grabbed onto the counter and stared into the mirror, breathing deeply.

Get a grip, she told herself. *Get a grip.*

★ ★ ★

There she went, running off again. Zach shook his head. He wanted this woman with a passion he'd never known. She was so damned beautiful, and kissing her was unlike anything he'd ever experienced. And he had experienced a lot. He was going to make love to her tonight. He had to. He'd been nursing a case of blue balls since he first laid eyes on her.

"Where did your date wander off to?"

Angelina's voice. Sheesh, just what he needed. He turned to face her.

"Ladies' room."

"You look a little lonely over here."

"I'm fine."

"Can we chat for a minute?"

"What about?" Zach checked his watch. He looked over Angelina's head to the door of the ballroom. Damn, Dusty wasn't going to take off again, was she?

"Oh, I don't know. Things."

"You'll have to be a little more specific, Angie." He sipped his Wild Turkey and the liquor burned his throat. Good stuff.

Angelina licked her lips and tugged on the lower one with her teeth as she eyed him. "Honestly, Zach, I had forgotten how handsome you are. You look great tonight."

"Thanks." She wanted something, and she wasn't going to get it.

She smiled coquettishly. "You're not going to return the compliment?"

"You always look great, Angie. You know that."

"It's nice to hear it sometimes."

"Okay. You look beautiful. Now what is it that you're after?"

"What makes you think I'm after anything?"

Zach chuckled under his breath. "We've known each other for years. You come over here, all flirty and fluttery. You want something."

"You do know me, don't you?" She curled her lips upward. "I thought we might be able to get together and talk."

"About what?"

"About us."

"There's no us, Angie. You broke up with me, remember?"

She sighed, her lips twisting into a pout. "Zach, I made a huge mistake letting you go."

"Nah, it wasn't a mistake. Things were never right between us." He checked his watch again and glanced to the door. No Dusty.

"We could try again. We could recapture it."

"Recapture what? There was never much more between us than friendship, no matter how hard we both tried."

"Of course there was. Don't you remember our lovemaking? That was phenomenal, Zach. Don't you ever wish we could go to bed again? Just once?"

"I'm sorry, Angie."

"My room's right upstairs."

"So's mine." Zach shifted his weight from one foot to the other. *Where the hell is she?*

"Okay, we'll go to yours."

"That's not what I meant."

"I'll make it worth your while. I haven't been able to think about anything except your luscious body."

"Christ, Angie. Shut the fuck up, will you?"

Dusty entered the ballroom and he silently thanked God.

"It's over, okay?"

"You'll change your mind."

Angelina walked away, swinging her considerable assets. She was a beauty, no doubt. Funny thing, though. Zach wasn't even slightly tempted. Instead, he couldn't take his eyes off the golden-haired goddess walking toward him. She looked a little flustered, but she was still the most delicious thing he'd ever seen.

"You all right, darlin'?"

"Fine." She plunked down in a chair. "I think I've had a little too much Wild Turkey, to tell you the truth. I don't usually drink hard stuff."

"Why did you tonight?"

She sighed. "I thought it would help me feel a little more at ease. You know, with Angelina and all."

"Angelina is nothing compared to you."

"That's sweet of you to say. But you and she—"

"That's over."

"I know. I just... Never mind."

"What is it, darlin'?"

Before she could answer, his brother Dallas and his wife approached the table. "Hey, Zach. Who's this?"

Trust Dallas to get straight to the point. "Dusty O'Donovan. Her pa used to work at the ranch back in the late eighties. You remember?"

"Can't say that I do."

"Sure you do. Her brother Sam was best friends with Chad."

"Sounds vaguely familiar." He held out his hand. "Dallas McCray."

"Nice to see you," Dusty said. "You look a lot like Zach, don't you? Except you're a little gray around the temples, and your nose is slightly larger. But still a very nice nose. And both your eyes are brown, of course." She hiccupped. "Excuse me."

Zach cringed as the blond woman next to his brother pursed her lips. What the hell was wrong with the bitch tonight? He thought Dusty's hiccup was charming. She was a little tipsy. Otherwise she probably wouldn't have mentioned Dallas's gray hair or his nose. But hell, it wasn't a damn secret. Dallas was still a chick magnet at thirty-five. Of course, Chelsea kept him on a short leash.

"This is my wife, Chelsea," Dallas said.

Chelsea held out her hand to Dusty. "Chelsea Beaumont McCray, of the Kennebunkport Beaumonts."

"Oh God," Zach said under his breath.

"Charmed," Dusty said.

Zach's smile widened. Oh, his little darlin' knew how to deal with Chelsea.

"That's a lovely outfit," Chelsea cooed to Dusty.

Damn. Dusty was sensitive about her appearance tonight. Why couldn't Chelsea leave well enough alone?

"Thank you," Dusty said sweetly. "You look splendid as well. I've never seen a lovelier shade of pink."

"It's Vera Wang," Chelsea said. "And it's not pink, it's bashful."

"Excuse me?"

"Bashful. The color?"

"Oh. Of course." Dusty put her hand on Zach's forearm.

A slight touch from her, and his loins ignited.

"It was lovely to meet you both, but I'm extremely tired. I worked with Zach's bull all day and—"

"What?" Dallas said, his tone incredulous. "You let her near that brute, Zach?"

"I was with her the whole time."

"You don't have the sense God gave a goose. If Pa were here—"

"Well, he's not. And you ain't him, Dallas. The big brother routine got old twenty years ago."

"I wasn't in any danger," Dusty said. "I'm good with bulls."

Chelsea eeked out a small disgusted sound. "I can't bear the beasts myself. They're ugly. And they smell."

"Only if they're not properly cared for," Dusty said.

"Pooh," Chelsea said. "You couldn't pay me to go near one of them."

"I'm betting if the price were right, you'd hang with the bulls," Zach said.

Dallas looked at him sternly but said nothing.

Chelsea laughed it off. "Maybe. If the price were the new suede outfit I saw today. Only four thousand three fifty."

Dusty visibly cringed.

"But tomorrow the vendor's having a sale," Chelsea continued. "Twenty-eight percent off in honor of his daughter's twenty-eighth birthday. So like a good girl, I'll wait until then to have it."

"I'm sure three thousand one thirty two is a fair price," Dusty said.

"Where'd that number come from?" Chelsea asked.

"It's twenty-eight percent off of your original price."

Chelsea's heavily lined eyes widened. "How'd you do that?"

"In my head."

"Dusty's a math whiz," Zach said.

Dallas pulled his cell phone out of his pocket and punched in a few numbers. "Damn. She's right."

"Of course she is," Zach said.

"What's the square root of seven hundred eighty-nine?" Dallas asked.

"I don't think..." Dusty began.

Zach watched her adorable face blush. Was she embarrassed by her ability?

"Ha," Chelsea said. "She can't do it."

"Twenty-eight point zero eight nine, rounded," Dusty said indignantly.

"Damn," Dallas said again.

"Are you some kind of idiot savant?" Chelsea asked.

Dusty's forehead wrinkled. "Excuse me?"

Zach gritted his teeth. "Damn, Dallas, can't you keep a lid on her mouth?"

"Dallas!" Chelsea whined.

"Jesus Christ, Chelsea," Dallas said. "That was just rude."

"You're not taking her side, are you? It was a valid

question, certainly not rude. You saw *Rain Man*."

"The woman's obviously not autistic. She's just good with numbers."

"Well, sorry." Chelsea flounced away, her bashful skirt rustling.

"What you see in her is beyond me." Zach looked down at Dusty's sad brown eyes. "I'm sorry."

"It's no big deal, Zach." Dusty looked away.

"Hell yes, it is," Zach said.

"Please accept my apology," Dallas said. "I know it's no excuse, but she's been in a mood all night."

"Fine," Dusty said, as she turned to Zach. "I'm exhausted, so would you mind excusing me?"

"I'll take you to your hotel, darlin'." Zach nodded to Dallas. "I'll see you tomorrow."

Zach wanted to take her up to his suite, but he had no intention of bedding her while she was upset about the run-in with Chelsea. And she had admitted to being tipsy. So much for his plan to make love to her tonight. He wanted to be sure she was completely sober and aware so she'd enjoy every mind-blowing minute.

Besides, he wanted her to trust him. If he took her back now, without pressuring her for more, maybe she'd stop running and tell him what was going on.

But he did give her a scalding good night kiss at her door. He was only human, after all.

★ ★ ★

"What'd you find out?"

Chelsea McCray licked her lips. "Not much more than you

already know. Her father worked at McCray Landing a while back. And she's some kind of weird mathematical genius."

Angelina curled her mouth into a snarl. "What's he see in her, anyway?"

"You've got me." Chelsea fidgeted with her small pink bag. "Pretty enough. But she's clearly nothing more than a step above common trailer trash."

"I'll get rid of her one way or another," Angelina said.

"Are you sure you want to marry into this family, anyway? Laurie's enough to make a saint swear, the way she coddles those three boys. She and I have never gotten along."

"But Chelsea, she and my mother are like this." Angelina held up two fingers side by side. "I'll get along fine with her. And I'll put in many good words for you."

"Honey, I don't need any good words. I couldn't care less if the shrew likes me. I have her firstborn. And his wallet. That's all I need."

"And I'll have her second born," Angelina vowed.

CHAPTER SIX

Zach was leaning against the fence surrounding the practice ring when Dusty, hauling her gear bag, arrived the next morning for her date with Diablo. In one hand, he held a brown paper bag, and in the other, a cup holder with two Starbucks cups.

"Hungry?" he asked.

"Starving, actually," she said.

"You feeling okay?"

"Yeah. I took two ibuprofen before I went to bed, just in case. I'm fine."

"Some coffee'll help too." He handed her a cup.

"Thank you. You're an angel."

"Definitely not." He laughed. "But I take good care of my own."

His own?

"I got you some breakfast, too." He pulled out a foil-wrapped sandwich and handed it to her.

"Thank you. But you don't need to feed me all the time. I can fend for myself, you know."

"Sure you can. But it gives me pleasure to feed you. I like how you eat."

"What do you mean by that?"

"I mean, you're not afraid to eat. When you're hungry, you eat like you're hungry."

Dusty raised an eyebrow. "Exactly how else would I eat?"

"Like most women. Eating like a bird, or not at all, in front of a man, and then bingeing when they get home. When I buy a woman a meal, I expect her to eat it. Otherwise it's a damn insult as far as I'm concerned."

"I guess you don't have to worry about me on that count," Dusty said. "I love to eat. Always have. I used to gorge on your ma's cookies."

"Yeah, I recall." The laugh lines at the edge of his eyes crinkled and made him even cuter.

Did he really remember her that well from all those years ago? "I was just a little girl. You can't possibly remember that much about me."

"Of course I do. You were always hanging around, running after Chad and Sam. You were cute as a button. Little tomboy, chasing grasshoppers and lizards. Animals flocked to you even then."

"I can't believe it."

"Why not? You remember me, don't you?"

"Mostly I remember you tormenting me."

"Aw, come on. I was just teasin'. We've been through all that."

"Yeah, I know."

"You're not going to hold that against me forever, are you, darlin'?"

She smiled at him. She couldn't help it. He looked so adorable. "No. I won't hold it against you."

He took her hand, entwined their fingers together, and pulled her into his arms. "There are a few things I'll let you hold against me, though. Your beautiful body, for instance." He kissed her cheek and nibbled his way to her lips.

"Oh, Zach." She sighed into his mouth. "If you start this

now..."

"Hmm?"

"If you start this now, I won't get to work with Diablo."

He pressed his mouth to hers, ran his tongue over first her bottom lip and then her top one. The sensation was like moist butterfly wings, and she felt it everywhere, especially...

Then his tongue was in her mouth, swirling. Unable to resist, she joined in the kiss, tasting him, feasting on him. Not able to get enough of him.

"Zach..."

"Hmm?"

"Diablo."

"To hell with Diablo."

He kissed her again.

She wasn't sure she could ever get enough of him. What was it about him? She had run from him, tried to hide. Tried to rid herself of the feelings she knew would lead only to heartache. She didn't want to run anymore. Didn't want to hide...

Sam was judging livestock all day and wouldn't be back until early evening. Her room was vacant. Oh, God...

"Zach?" Her tone was breathless, hoarse.

"Yeah, darlin'?"

"Take me to my hotel."

He grabbed her hand and they raced to his pickup.

★ ★ ★

They stood outside the door to her room while she fished for her key card.

"You sure about this, darlin'?"

"Yeah, yeah." She had a hard time breathing. "I'm sure, Zach. I want this."

Zach grabbed her purse from her. "Where the hell is that damn key?"

He found it, pushed it in the slot, and pulled her into the room, shutting the door and pushing her body against it. His hardness protruded through his jeans and poked into her belly. She wanted to touch him everywhere, lick him everywhere. She wanted to rip his clothes off and her own, and get down and dirty right there on the hotel rug.

"You're so beautiful." He cupped her face in his hands. "You have the longest eyelashes I've ever seen." He pushed his erection into her. "Do you feel that?"

"Yes."

"Feel how much I want you. How much I hunger for you."

"Yes, yes." Her breathing was unsteady, her pulse wild.

"Do you want me?"

"God, yes. Yes."

"Say it, darlin'. Say you want me."

"I want you."

His mouth, reckless and possessive, claimed hers. His strong arms enveloped her and carried her to the bed. He laid her down gently and unbuttoned her shirt. He moved slowly, letting his fingers linger as he tantalized each inch of flesh. She squirmed as tiny flames ignited every place he touched her. She wanted to rip her shirt off and move things along.

When he finally exposed her breasts and lavished his attention on them, she wanted even more. She wanted to be naked. Naked under his touch. She wriggled and groaned, whispering his name.

"Please," she said, and found herself repeating the word.

"Please what, darlin'?"

"I...don't know."

"Do you want me to touch you?"

"Yes, please."

"Here?" He cupped her breast, lightly running his thumb over her taut nipple.

She shuddered.

"Here?" He grazed his fingers lightly over her belly, circling them around her navel.

She squirmed.

"Here?" He unsnapped her jeans and ran his fingers under the waistband.

Tremors surged through her. "Oh yes," she said, sighing.

He slowly unzipped her jeans, eased his hand inside her panties, and found a sensitive spot that sent her writhing.

"Here?" His voice was hoarse, needy.

"God, Zach. Yes."

His strong callused fingers toyed with her delicate folds. Heady. Wonderful. When he removed his hands, she whimpered. He swirled his tongue around his fingers, tasting her juices.

"Mmm. You're sweet as a peach."

He plunged his fingers back inside her panties. He smoothed over her folds again, and she gasped when one thick finger slid inside her.

"Tight. So tight," he whispered. "Damn, you're going to be a sweet fuck."

His coarse words should have astonished her, but instead they turned her on, made her prickly and moist. Sweet fuck indeed. She wanted to be his sweet fuck. Sweeter than anything he'd ever had. His finger stretched her, filled her, stroked her.

He moved in and out, around and around, finally settling on a place that drove her mad with wanting. She moaned, wailing his name, begging and pleading.

"Darlin', I want to make love to you."

"Yes, Zach. Yes. Make love to me."

"Oh, yeah. I'm going to make love to you like no one ever has before."

If only Dusty hadn't chosen that moment to turn her head. She had wanted his lips on her ear, her neck. So she twisted to the right, her gaze landing on the night table.

The phone sitting there.

The message light was flashing.

The red pulse of it consumed her, took over her heartbeat, her breath, her mind. A buzzing sound, surrounded by white noise, echoed in her head to the beat of the flashing light.

★ ★ ★

What had he done wrong?

Zach stalked out to his pickup, bewildered. She had jumped off the bed and zipped up her jeans. Her beautiful breasts, reddened from his kisses and resting on her chest, had jiggled between the two sides of her unbuttoned shirt as she kicked him out. Unceremoniously. Thoroughly. No explanation.

Was it because he had said she'd be a sweet fuck? He had meant it in a loving way. He didn't consider what he wanted to do with her to be merely fucking. She knew that, didn't she?

She was so perfect. So beautiful. So tight and wet. He had never wanted anything, anyone, the way he wanted her. And not only because she was attractive. He liked her as a person.

He liked that she loved animals. He liked that she was so dedicated to her ranch and to her brother. He liked that she could out eat a lot of men he knew, and that she wasn't afraid to do it. He liked that she could do complicated calculations in her head. He liked that she was so determined to connect with Diablo. He liked that she was intelligent and brave.

He liked *her*. He really, really liked her.

He couldn't remember ever liking a woman this much. It wasn't...*love* was it? Nah, couldn't be. Zach McCray didn't fall in love.

But he wasn't about to give up. Dusty O'Donovan would soon find out getting rid of Zach McCray wasn't so easy. He would get her to open up to him. And he'd get her into bed. One way or another.

He stepped out of his cold shower to Mozart playing on his cell phone. "Yeah?"

"Zach." The deep voice was so like his own.

Shit. Not Dallas. Not now. The only person he wanted to talk to less was Dallas's stupid wife.

"What is it?"

"We need to talk."

"I can't imagine what about."

"About your new girlfriend."

"I'm pretty sure that falls under the heading of 'none of your damn business,' Dallas."

"I'm concerned about you."

"You stopped being concerned about me the day I started walking."

"That's not fair, Zach."

Zach snorted. "Sure enough is. When you weren't playing pseudo father, you were ignoring Chad and me. So why should

I listen to you now?"

"Because I'm your brother, and I want what's best for you."

"And in your opinion that's not Dusty?"

"Not by a long shot. She's after your money, Zach."

"That's Chelsea talking, not you. Not that I ever gave a damn what she thought, but after her performance last night, I sure as hell ain't interested in her opinion."

"Damn it, I'm not the whipped lemming you and Chad like to think I am. I agree she was out of line. But this has nothing to do with Chelsea."

"Right," Zach scoffed.

"She's not the right woman for you, Zach."

"You don't know anything about me, especially not what kind of woman I want."

"She's using you."

"She's a sweet girl, and I don't think she even knows how to use someone."

"Christ, you just met her."

"So? You and Chelsea knew each other for—what?—three weeks before you were engaged?"

"That's different. Chelsea's different. She's—"

"From the Kennebunkport Beaumonts. Yeah, I know. A nice Yale girl. And I use the term nice loosely. Very loosely."

Dallas continued. "Where did Dusty go to school?"

"Don't know. Don't care."

"Did she even go to school?"

"Yeah." For one year, but Dallas didn't need to know that.

"I don't want to see you get hurt."

"Then don't try to keep me away from Dusty." He cleared his throat. "This conversation is over, Dallas." He hit End and tossed the phone on his bed. He dressed quickly and headed back to the stock show grounds.

* * *

"That's right, sweetheart," Dusty crooned to Diablo. "No one's going to hurt you."

The bull was anxious. Dusty could sense it. He had fed on a bale of hay and drunk several gallons of water, and although he should be relaxed after a huge meal, something was bothering him. Was it her? Was it because Zach wasn't with her?

She knew how Zach would react when he found out she had sneaked in to see Diablo, but she had needed it.

She closed her eyes and concentrated for several moments. Then she walked around to his head and looked into his eyes. "Relax, relax," she said, trying to soothe him. She began the lullaby, her gaze never straying from his.

She sang it through three times before the bull began to relax. She reached out to touch his cheek. "Yes, that's a good boy," she said, stroking gently. His short hair was bristly yet soft. She caressed it, and then held her hand still, continuing to gaze into the animal's brown eyes. "You're not such a brute, are you?" She sang again, moving her hand slowly down to stroke his nose. He snorted, but she remained calm and left her hand where it was. Within minutes, the bull's body loosened, and she saw gentleness in his eyes.

Timidly, she reached out her other hand, but the boom of a flare gun sounded at that exact moment, startling Diablo. He snorted menacingly and shuffled his front paw on the dirt beneath him. Then he bucked his head and pushed Dusty backward. She landed on her behind.

"Damn, damn!" She leaned back against a bale of hay, her rear end stinging from the fall. She cursed the gun that had ruined her connection with the bull, and she cursed herself for not being better able to control him.

Why did I think I could control such a strong, beautiful animal? I can't even control my own body, my own blood. Damn the bull, damn the blood, damn everything in the universe!

The tears she'd tried so hard not to shed finally fell.

★ ★ ★

Zach found her there.

Curled up next to Diablo's pen in a fetal position, weeping.

He didn't try to talk to her, just sat her up and brushed the dirt and hay from her face and body. He pulled a red bandana out of his pocket, wiped the tears from her cheeks, and covered her nose and urged her to blow. He lifted her in his arms, carried her to his pickup, set her inside, and drove her to his hotel.

"It's okay, darlin'. Come on." He helped her out of the passenger side and led her up to his suite of rooms on the top floor of the hotel. He nudged her inside and through the living area to the bedroom. Gently, he pushed her down onto a chair.

"What can I do to help you?"

No response.

"Would you like a shower?"

She shook her head.

"A bath?"

She nodded.

"Okay."

A bath. He could handle that. As long as he didn't have

to look at her naked. She needed gentleness and caring, not a horny cowboy.

"You just sit there for a few minutes. I'll get it ready for you." He walked to the mini-bar, pulled out a can of Sprite, opened it, and handed it to her. "Here. You need to drink something."

She nodded and took a sip. Good. At least she was responding a little better now.

He went into the bathroom and ran a warm bath, adding something called Honey Milk that he found by the sink. It smelled nice, feminine. He hoped Dusty would like it.

When he was finished, he called to her but she didn't respond, so he went to fetch her. "Come on. It's ready." He took her hand, pulled her out of the chair, and led her into the bathroom. "I'll wait outside," he said.

But she pulled him to her. "Stay," she whispered. "Please."

She pulled the band out of her hair and unwound the braid. Silky waves fell around her shoulders. She unbuttoned and removed her blouse, unhooked her bra, and revealed those beautiful peachy breasts.

She stood there, naked from the waist up. Zach was puzzled. He waited for her to move, but she didn't. How was he supposed to handle this? His desire for her was like lightning in his veins, but she needed him to be calm, to take care of her. He took a deep breath, lifted her onto the counter, and pulled off her boots. "This okay?"

She nodded, so he pulled her down and unbuckled her belt and unsnapped her jeans. She shimmied out of them and stood before him wearing only a pair of lacy bikinis. His cock stiffened, but she was so distraught. He had to control himself. He touched her hips—God, the fire in his loins—and gently eased the panties downward. Ah, sweet golden curls, beautiful pink woman. He willed himself to soften, without much luck, and he lifted her and placed her in the tub.

Her sigh was like a gentle breeze as she leaned back. He turned to leave.

"Zach."

Her voice cut right into his heart.

He turned, and the sight of her beautiful body soaking in the fragrant water about undid him. When she held out her arms to him, he thought he might melt into a puddle right there on the bathroom floor.

"You want me?"

She nodded.

"In the tub. With you?"

She nodded again. If only she would smile that sweet smile, curve those cherry lips upward. He couldn't take advantage of her like this.

"Please, Zach."

He wasn't made of stone. Well, one part of him was at the moment. Within seconds, his clothes were in disarray on the floor. He stepped in behind her and nestled her into his chest.

He wanted to help her, to comfort her, to take away whatever was hurting her. So why didn't his dick understand that? Her beautiful body felt perfect against him, like she was created to fit into him. The Honey Milk softened the water, and the slickness of her delicate skin against his chest...

He couldn't hide his arousal. He would control himself, but his erection was there to stay. He hoped it didn't bother her.

She seemed oblivious. He was hyper-conscious of her breathing. Every rise and fall of her chest sank her more deeply into him. He reached to the side, grabbed a bar of soap, lathered it between his palms, and spread the silky suds onto her arms, caressing her lightly. She sighed, a delicate flutter against his arms, so he lathered up some more and ran it over her breasts, pausing for a moment to squeeze them lightly.

"That's nice," she whispered, turning her head slightly. He lowered his mouth to her cheek and gave her a chaste kiss.

She surprised him when she turned around and hugged her cheek to his hard chest. When she wrapped her arms around him, he exhaled slowly, hoping his hardness didn't disturb her relaxation. They stayed in that position for a while, until the water became lukewarm.

Zach kissed the top of her golden head. "The water's cooling off, darlin'. Do you want to get out now?"

She nodded, sat up, and stepped out of the tub. He stepped behind her and wrapped her in a towel. He dried her and sheathed her in a fluffy white robe provided by the hotel. After drying himself and donning another robe, he led her to the bed and laid her down. She curled onto her side and closed her eyes. He lay down behind her, spoon fashion, and wrapped her in his arms. Soon the heavy breathing of her slumber calmed him, and he fell asleep.

★ ★ ★

He awoke to her caresses. She was touching his face, running her slender fingers over his cheekbones, his nose, his lips. He puckered his lips and kissed her fingers.

"Thank you for taking care of me," she said.

"You're welcome. I was glad to do it." He cupped her cheek and ran his thumb over her delicate skin. "Do you want to tell me what's bothering you?"

She shook her head and then leaned down and brushed her cherry lips across his. "I don't want to talk," she said. "I just want to make love."

Zach's heart leaped, and another part of his anatomy responded, as well. "Are you sure?"

She nodded. "I'm sure. And I'm sorry I ran from you so many times. I was frightened. But I'm not anymore. I want you."

"Don't you think we should talk first?" *Talk? A beautiful woman wants you and you're trying to talk?*

"We can talk later." Her voice sounded sweet, yet sultry. "Right now I want you inside me."

Jesus, she didn't have to ask twice. He sighed as he pushed her beautiful golden waves out of her eyes. "Darlin', I want you so much."

"I want you, too."

"Come here." He pulled her to him and kissed her beautiful mouth, running his tongue over the seam of her lips and coaxing them open. When her tongue darted out and touched his, he nearly came right there. The sweet spiciness of her mouth, the silky texture, the scent of her hair, of her arousal. He kissed her with a strange mixture of reverence and a strong passion he had never known. He was going to make this good for her. So good.

He continued to kiss her as he caressed her neck, her shoulders. "You're so beautiful," he whispered. "I've never seen anyone more lovely."

Dusty closed her eyes and leaned her head back. Zach nuzzled her neck, her pulse point, inhaling her sweet fragrance. "Come here, darlin'," he said and pulled her down on the bed. He pushed the robe from her lovely body and removed his own.

He leaned over her and kissed her again, thrusting his tongue into her mouth with urgency. Taking. Giving. She responded with a frenzy.

Yes, she wanted this as much as he did.

He broke from her mouth and licked his way down to her beautiful breasts, circling each pebbled nipple, biting and tugging. Her sighs and moans fueled him as he worshiped her. When her nipples were deep ruby from his attention, he kissed her belly, pushed his tongue into her navel, and buried his nose in her golden curls. Oh, the sweet scent of her arousal, muskiness mixed with fresh apples. He could drown in it. He moved his mouth just a hair's breadth farther down and kissed her swollen folds.

Her sex glistened with cream. He almost felt he could be satisfied just to look at her.

Almost.

Then he dove in.

Sweet, sweet ecstasy. She made such sexy, exquisite noises as he feasted. She urged him on, told him how much she loved what he was doing. Her folds were soft and silky against his tongue. He brought her to the edge several times before he let her come, and then he slid two fingers inside her and felt each and every spasm as she shouted his name.

"Oh my God," Dusty said breathlessly. "That's the most amazing thing I've ever felt."

The most she'd spoken since he'd found her. Was it possible that she had never experienced an orgasm? Not likely.

Zach crawled atop her body and kissed her slowly. "Let me come inside you, darlin'," he rasped.

"Yes, please."

"I'll be right back."

"No. Don't go."

"It'll just be a minute. I need to get a condom."

"No. No. I can't get pregnant. And I don't have any...other issues. Please, just you. Just you inside me.

Sweet God, she was on the pill. And she was clean. Instinct told him to trust her. The thought of sheathing himself in that tight body of hers with no barriers made his erection swell even bigger.

"Are you sure?" he asked.

"Yes. Yes, I'm sure."

"I'm clean, too, I promise," he whispered. He positioned himself at her entrance and plunged inside.

Her shocked gasp surprised him momentarily, but he was overcome with pleasure at her tightness, her silkiness, her sweet suction hugging him. "Oh, darlin', you feel so good."

She squirmed and arched closer to him, moaning. Her breathy sobs threatened his control. He wanted her to climax again, but he wasn't sure how long he could hold out. Deftly, he reached between their sweaty bodies and found her clit, wet with her nectar. He circled it with his fingers in tandem with his thrusts. When her walls clenched around him, he let go and groaned her name as he spilled into her.

CHAPTER SEVEN

Dusty awoke, nestled in the crook of Zach's arm. He was breathing steadily, and his eyes—those amazing, beautiful, unique eyes—fluttered beneath the lids. She smiled. He was dreaming.

She moved gingerly, the soreness between her legs more pronounced than she had expected. Perhaps he had been larger than normal. Not that she would have known the difference.

Absolutely wonderful. A mistake, of course.

But a wonderful mistake.

She got up quietly and shuffled into the bathroom. Gazing into the mirror, she was startled. Her hair was a mass of waves, yet it looked sexy. Her cheeks were flushed and her nipples a deep crimson. She looked well used and well loved. She felt the same.

Looking down to the triangle between her legs she noticed a few rust-colored smudges on her inner thighs.

Her virgin's blood.

She moistened a washcloth in warm water and cleansed herself. The warm dampness soothed the sting of her tissues.

"Darlin'?"

She looked up. Zach stood in the doorway, naked and regal. Oh, he was beautiful. His broad shoulders glimmered in the fluorescent light of the vanity, the lines of his muscles a pleasure to behold, and the patch of dark hair on his chest was so rugged. So manly. Between his legs, his sex hung loosely, surrounded by a nest of black curls. And those eyes... She wanted to melt into them.

"Darlin'?" He spoke again. "I didn't hurt you, did I?"

"No." Warmth crept up her neck.

"That wasn't your—"

"My first time." She rinsed out the cloth. "Yeah."

"I didn't know."

"I know. It's okay."

"But how? Why?"

She turned and walked into his arms. "I never wanted anyone enough. Until now."

He kissed the top of her head. "I'm honored."

Okay, now she was embarrassed. "It's no big deal."

"Are you kidding?" He grasped her shoulders, pushed her away, and bored his eyes into hers. "It's a huge deal. And if I had known, I could have made it better for you."

"No, you couldn't have. It was perfect. Thank you."

"Aw, hell, I'm the one who should be thanking you. You gave me a priceless gift. I'll always treasure it, darlin'."

Dusty didn't know what to say, so she said nothing.

"And it'll be better next time. Just wait and see." He winked at her.

Of course, there wouldn't be a next time, but she didn't want to tell him that yet. She wanted to hold him and pretend nothing else in the world existed.

His voice breached her thoughts. "If you weren't, you know, active sexually, why are you on the pill?"

"What? Oh, yeah, the pill." Dusty cleared her throat. "Irregular periods."

"Oh."

"Let's go back to bed," she said.

"You're sore. We should wait—"

"I didn't mean it that way. I just want to lie with you. In your arms."

He smiled down at her, took her hand, and led her back to the bed. She snuggled into him, sighing. "You smell good."

"Like honey and milk?" His eyes twinkled.

"Kind of."

"That's what I put in the bath."

Dusty giggled softly. "Somehow you don't seem the milk bath type."

"What a man'll do for his woman." He squeezed her breast playfully.

His woman. Wow. She did like the sound of it. If only it could be. "It's not just honey and milk. You smell fresh, and musky."

"That's you, darlin'. I smell like you."

"Oh." She heated.

"It's the smell of sex. Of our scents mingled together." He inhaled deeply. "There's no sweeter perfume."

She breathed in and had to agree with him.

"Dusty?"

"Yeah?" She winced. She already knew him well enough to know that when he used her name, instead of calling her darling, something was up.

"What was going on with you earlier?"

"I'm hungry." She wasn't, but she had to change the subject.

"I'll call room service."

"No, I should go... I'm barrel racing tomorrow."

"Oh. Shoot."

"What?"

"I'm one of the judges for the barrel racing. I guess I'll have to disqualify myself."

"Why? You're not even a real judge. There's no subjectivity in barrel racing."

"Still—" He pulled her close and pressed his lips to hers. "I can hardly be impartial when I'm sleeping with one of the contestants."

"There's no impartiality. You just record the time and watch if any barrels get knocked over. I trust you to be fair." She smiled. "I'm going to win, anyway. Sydney Buchanan's the only one who has come close to my record time, and I already know I can beat her."

He kissed her again. "Just the same, I'm recusing myself. But I'll be there to cheer you on."

"You don't have to."

"Woman, I *want* to. Now if you're hungry, I'm calling room service, and we'll have dinner together up here. And we'll *talk*."

He stood and went into the living area.

Talk? Why did he want to talk? Weren't men supposed to hate talking?

He came back in with the room service menu and tossed it on the bed. "Order whatever you want."

"I'm not really hungry."

"Damn it, Dusty, you just said you were."

"Oh. Right." She had to get out of here. "I should go, though. I haven't given Regina a workout today, and we're competing tomorrow."

"You know as well as I do that a day off before a competition is good for an animal."

"Not everyone subscribes to that viewpoint."

"But I'm willing to bet you do. With your love of animals."

She sighed. He was right, of course. "I should get back though. I'll need a good night's sleep..."

"Dusty, it's six o'clock, and we spent half the afternoon sleeping."

"I need to call Sam."

"So call him."

"I don't have a cell phone." She grimaced at the look of surprise on Zach's face.

He pointed to the phone on the nightstand. "So?"

"Fine." She quickly dialed the hotel and left Sam a message.

When she was finished, Zach took the phone from her.

"This is suite twenty-five hundred. I'll have the Chateaubriand for two, please, with green beans and garlic mashed potatoes. Oysters on the half-shell for an appetizer." A pause. "Yeah, that'd be great. And a chocolate soufflé for dessert." He started to put the phone down, and then spoke again. "You still there? A bottle of your best Bordeaux. Thanks."

Dusty's mouth dropped open. He had just ordered about three hundred dollars' worth of food. That was her and Sam's grocery budget for a month. At least, it had been while they were saving for this trip to Denver. The steak dinner the previous evening must have set him back about a hundred and fifty, but this was plain crazy.

"Uh, Zach?"

"Hmm?"

"You don't need to spend that much money on dinner for me."

"For you?" He grinned and touched her chin, forcing her to look at him. "I thought I might eat some, too."

"Of course, but—"

"You said you're hungry, and you need to eat a good solid meal so you're at your best for competition tomorrow."

"And the wine?"

"Goes great with the meat." He gave her a lazy half-smile.

"What I don't need is a hangover."

"You won't have one. I'll take good care of you tonight. I promise."

Dusty sighed and smiled. Why not share a meal with him? She had shared her body, and she had no regrets. She wanted to let him take care of her. She wasn't ready for it all to end.

"You want another bath?" he asked. "It'll help the soreness."

It did sound heavenly. "Yeah, but I need to wash my hair. So I'd better take a shower."

"Nah, a bath." He grinned at her. "And *I'll* wash your hair."

Now why in the world did the thought of Zach washing her hair completely turn her on?

"Only if I get to wash yours." The idea of threading her fingers through his black silk thrilled her.

"I won't turn that down, darlin'." He started for the bathroom. "I'll run the bath and call you when it's ready."

"Mmm," Dusty purred, and then lay back on the bed. She missed him already, and he was only in the bathroom. She ran her hands over her breasts, cupping them, squeezing them, making her nipples harden. She moved one hand down to her triangle of curls, imagining Zach's silky head between her legs, his hot mouth pleasuring her.

"Now that's a lovely sight."

Zach stood in the doorway between the bathroom and the bedroom, his eyes smoldering.

Dusty warmed and redness crept to her breasts. She

stilled her hands.

Zach grinned. "Your bath is ready, darlin'. Though I think I'd rather join you."

Though embarrassed, she couldn't help but chuckle. How she wished she could forget everything about her life and stay here in this room forever, making sweet love to this phenomenal man.

"Come on," he said. "I promised you a scalp massage."

"A scalp massage? I just need my hair washed."

"There's more to hair washing than shampoo and conditioner." He winked. "It's an erotic art."

She smiled. He was so damned adorable. "An erotic art, huh? This an invention of yours?"

"Yeah. As of five minutes ago. Come on."

Erotic art, indeed. Zach's strong and talented hands reduced Dusty to a pool of jelly by the time he had rinsed and conditioned her. As an added benefit, her hair felt extraordinarily clean.

"Your hair is beautiful," he said. "And so long."

"I've been growing it out for a while. Almost five years."

"You used to wear it short?"

"Yeah. Real short, actually."

"I can't imagine that look on you."

"Trust me, it's not flattering. Luckily my hair grows really fast." She threaded her fingers through his black waves. "Now I get to do you."

"Oh, I'd love that, darlin'." He gave her a playful smirk. "But I'll settle for you washing my hair for now."

She gave him a good-natured splash and lathered his thick, dark hair. Her hands weren't as strong as Zach's, so she hoped her scalp massage felt as good to him as his had to her.

His soft moans indicated she was successful.

When they had washed and caressed each other's bodies and the water turned lukewarm, they toweled off and dressed in the fluffy robes.

"Feel better now?" Zach touched her gently between her legs.

"It never felt bad," she said, "but yes, it's better now."

Their dinner arrived soon after, and Dusty ate heartily, allowing the food to replenish her body. Eating with Zach was becoming a habit that would be difficult to break. Though not as difficult as the other habit she had just begun with him.

The wine he had ordered complemented the meal, and Dusty was nearly too full to try the chocolate soufflé, but Zach insisted.

"Oh," she groaned. "I don't need to eat for another week." She looked around the room. "Where are my clothes, Zach? I need to get going."

"They were filthy with hay and dirt. I sent them down to the laundry."

"Oh, no. When will they be ready?"

"In the morning."

"Great. What do you propose I wear back to my hotel? This robe and a pair of your boxers?"

"Sure." He reached into a dresser drawer and threw her a pair of red silk shorts. "You'll look adorable in these."

Okay, the thought of putting his silk boxers on her bare skin had possibilities...but no. "I'm serious, Zach. I have to go."

He leered at her. "You'll just have to spend the night here, darlin'." He pulled her into a hug.

"I can't."

"Why not?"

"Well, Sam..."

"I think I'd rather it just be you and me," Zach teased.

"You know what I mean."

"Why do you need to leave, Dusty? Don't you want to be with me?"

"It's not that..." *God, no, it isn't that.*

"Please stay with me. I want to hold you and wake up next to you."

Her heart melted inside her chest. What could it hurt? One night. One wonderful, incredible night in the arms of a wonderful, incredible man. What a perfect memory to get her through the rough times.

"Okay, Zach. I'll stay. But I need to be at the barrel racing competition by nine sharp to warm up."

"Yes, ma'am." He saluted.

"Be serious."

"I am serious. I'll get you there, and I'll be your loudest cheerer."

She smiled. He was so, so handsome. "Zach?"

"What, darlin'?"

"Let's go to bed."

"I don't know," he teased. "You may have to twist my arm a little."

Dusty smiled and handed him the red boxers. "Put these on, and I'll make it worth your while."

"I guess I can manage that."

Zach pulled the boxers over his hips and Dusty gulped, shuddering. "You're incredible," she said. "You should be an underwear model."

His wide grin sparkled, and two rosy spots appeared on his cheeks.

"I haven't embarrassed the great Zach McCray, have I?" Dusty slowly ran a finger around the waistband of the boxers.

His response to her was immediate. The head of his cock peeked out from the fly of the shorts. "You're killin' me."

"But what a way to go."

"You said it."

"Now, what should we do?" Dusty grinned.

"Whatever you want. I'm yours for the night." He brushed his lips against hers.

"What do you want to do?" she asked.

"Honestly?"

"Yeah."

"I'd like to make love to you again and show you how good it can be. If I'd known it was your first time..."

"We've been through that. I loved it."

"I'm glad. But this time'll be better. I promise."

"Okay." Dusty slipped her arm around his back and stroked the cheek of his bottom through the silk. She smiled when he groaned. "Make love to me, Zach. Do whatever you want to me."

"Oh, darlin'"—his sexy voice flowed over her, into her—"I want to show you everything, teach you everything, experience ecstasy with you."

His mouth found hers, and he took it gently, easing her open and kissing her with his lips, his teeth, his tongue. Dusty moaned as her skin tingled, her heart throbbed. If she lived to be a hundred, she'd never tire of Zach's kisses.

He gently nudged her onto the bed and covered his body with hers, continuing his assault on her mouth. His erection pushed through the red silk into her thigh. She moved her hands down the strong sinewy musculature of his back and eased the sleek fabric down. He wriggled out of the boxers and covered her body with his again. Dusty loved the feeling of his weight on her. Of his hard muscled perfection blanketing her with warmth and joy. They continued to kiss, their lips meshing together in white heat. When Zach finally left her mouth, Dusty was panting.

He kissed a trail over her cheeks, her nose, and kissed her eyelids as gently as a butterfly. He nibbled on her ear and whispered to her how beautiful she was, how hard she made him, how much he wanted her. She ran her hands over his shoulders and neck, his muscular back, the firm male shape of him a pleasure to touch.

"You're so damned beautiful," he said. "I can't get enough of you."

He continued to trail fluttery kisses down her neck, over her chest, and then lifted his head for a moment to stare at her breasts. "Beautiful," he said. "So beautiful."

As he sucked a nipple between his lips, Dusty gasped and writhed, tangled her fingers in his silky black hair and urged him on. He nipped and bit at her, tugging on her nipple.

"The other one, Zach. Please, the other one."

Zach released her nipple with a soft pop and turned his attention to the other. Was it possible to climax just from breast stimulation? Before she could find out, he was licking her belly, pausing at her blond curls.

"So beautiful," he said again and buried his nose in her. "So sweet." When his tongue darted out and flicked her, she bucked beneath him. He spread her legs and gazed at her. "Hold still, darlin'. I'm gonna show you a real good time."

"Oh, God." Dusty hardly recognized her own voice.

Zach clamped his mouth down on her and thrust out his

tongue, kissing her as though he were kissing her mouth. His tongue swirled over her slick folds, licking them, tugging them between his teeth. Then he pushed his tongue into her opening again.

Dusty wanted to squirm, but he held her still. He licked her, sucked her, pushed her thighs forward, and slid his tongue over the sensitive skin of her buttocks.

"Zach..." she said tentatively.

"Hush, darlin'," he said. "Just enjoy it."

"Zach..."

He looked up, his chin and cheeks shining with her juices. "Yeah?"

"If you don't come inside me soon I think I'll go crazy."

His gorgeous smile warmed her. "I *want* to make you crazy."

"My God—"

He thrust two fingers inside her, and within seconds he had found a secret spot that made her explode inside. The orgasm shattered her and took her off the bed, seemed to levitate her over the mountains. She heard herself screaming his name. When she finally came back to earth, he began again, sucking her and massaging the inside of her with his clever fingers. Soon she slid back into euphoria.

Dusty lost count of how many times she climaxed. "Zach," she pleaded. "No more. No more. I want *you* now. *You.*"

"One more, darlin'," he said. "Fly for me. I want to make you soar."

With his words she burst outward, outside her body once more. She was flying, just like he said. So high above the snowcapped mountains. Soaring like an eagle. Her body spasmed with the flight, shaking, trembling, the physical sensations mixed with heady emotion. When Zach lifted his mouth from her, she plummeted downward, still convulsing against his fingers, which he circled slowly inside her.

Limp and sated, she closed her eyes as Zach trailed his lips and tongue up her belly, her breasts, her neck. When he got to her mouth he stopped, leaving no more than a few inches between them.

"Open your eyes." The breath from his words was a soft caress against her lips. "Look at me."

Her eyelids fluttered as she obeyed his command and gazed into his beautiful unique eyes. So wonderful, this man. She expected him to kiss her, but he didn't. They just stared into each other's eyes. Her heart melted, her skin tingled, her mind melded with his. And just as she thought their very souls had joined, he took her mouth with his and thrust into her.

The sweet caress of his tongue, the urgent stabs of his cock, his hard body against hers—Dusty thought she had died and gone to heaven. She couldn't imagine being closer to anyone. Ever.

As he joined with her, made love to her, she felt they were one body. And when she climaxed, he groaned and pushed into her, filling her. Zach had been right. It *was* better—perfect and amazing and absolute bliss.

He rolled them to the side, his sex still embedded inside her, and pulled her into his arms.

CHAPTER EIGHT

Dusty took a deep breath and smoothed Regina's soft black mane. Sydney Buchanan had made good time, but hadn't hit her personal best of 14.1. Dusty could still take first, but it would require intense concentration. She had to win. She needed the money. Especially now.

One more deep breath, and then she kicked into high gear. Her braid slapped her back as she and Regina crossed the electric eye and raced toward the first barrel. Dusty gritted her teeth as she set Regina up to turn the first barrel without knocking it over. Then, in a whirlwind, the centrifugal force invigorating her, Dusty took Regina around the first barrel perfectly. Pursing her lips, she looked straight ahead and galloped toward the second, taking Regina around in the opposite direction. Excellent. One more to go. Running toward the backside of the arena, she aimed toward the third and final barrel, the sweet rush of adrenaline empowering her.

Yes, yes, she was doing it. Regina was in fine form as Dusty rounded the last barrel.

"Yee haw!" she heard from the stands, and she looked up briefly.

This wasn't new to her. She often looked in the stands near the end of a race. It energized her to see the crowd cheering, and she was always able to keep her concentration.

But not this time.

Because she saw Zach, her Zach, in the arms of Angelina

Bay. His lips were on hers.

Within a microsecond, Regina had knocked down the final barrel.

Dusty forced herself into the zone and headed for home, a straight shot back down the center of the arena. She had done well, and she could still take the gold. If only—

Crossing the electric eye, she noted her time.

13.4 seconds.

A personal best for her.

But she wouldn't win. Knocking over the barrel would cost her a five second penalty. Her time would be calculated at 18.4 seconds. Sydney would take first at 14.9 seconds. Dusty wouldn't even place.

She fought back tears as she left the arena and took care of Regina. She could cry later. Right now, her horse needed her.

Standing beside her horse in her assigned stall, Dusty brushed out Regina's mane and curried her coat. "It wasn't your fault, sweetheart," she crooned. "It was me. All me."

"Tough break."

She looked up to see a tall man with tousled brown hair. Handsome. No Zach, but handsome nonetheless. And familiar. She had seen him before.

"It happens," Dusty replied.

"That's a fine mare you got there," he said.

"Regina's the best. Never knocked over a barrel before today."

"I can believe it. She was amazing. So were you."

"Yeah, well, not quite amazing enough."

"As you say, it happens." He held out his hand. "I'm Harper, by the way. Harper Bay."

Of course, she had seen him at the Bay party. Angelina's

brother. Zach's almost-brother-in-law. After today, they'd be on the road to relations again. She took his outstretched hand. "Dusty O'Donovan."

"My sister mentioned you. I'm sorry we didn't get to meet the other night. I hear you're seeing Zach McCray?"

Not anymore. "No."

"Oh." His face brightened. "I came in here because I have a proposition for you. But if you're not involved with McCray, would you like to discuss it over coffee?"

"Depends on what it is."

"Come to coffee and you'll find out."

He smiled at her. A nice, genuine smile. Was this guy really related to that Mary Ann wannabe?

"Look, Harper"—Dusty continued to curry Regina—"you seem like a nice man, and I appreciate the invitation. But I'm not in the mood at the moment. I just lost a race I should have won. I'm sure you understand."

"Yeah, I understand." He looked at her, his eyes rife with kindness. "Hell, I've been there myself. We all have."

"I'm sure. If you'll excuse me."

"Can we talk here?"

Dusty sighed. Why not? "What's on your mind?"

"Well, besides you..." His brown eyes glimmered. "Your horse."

"What about my horse?"

"She's the finest barrel racer I've seen in some time, and my sister's birthday is coming up. She's just getting into racing."

"Angelina races? I thought she said she wasn't involved in the rodeo."

"Not Angelina. My younger sister, Caitlyn. Her sweet sixteen is next month, and my pa and I have been looking around for a horse for her. Yours is the finest I've seen."

"Sorry." Dusty turned away. "She's not for sale."

"I'd pay top dollar."

Dusty inhaled sharply and met Harper's gaze. "Just how much is top dollar?"

"How's forty K sound?"

Dusty shook her head. "No. Sorry."

"Okay. Fifty."

"Sorry again."

"Seventy-five is as high as I can go."

Dusty gasped. This was Regina, her friend and comrade. How could she let Regina go? But seventy-five thousand dollars... It wouldn't save the ranch but it would be a start. She had just blown the barrel race. Money was more important now than ever.

"Your sister would take care of her?"

"Heck, yeah. She loves animals, especially horses."

"I don't mean to be rude, but she's not like..."

"Angelina?" Harper chuckled. "No, Catie's nothing like Angie. I take it you don't care for my big sister?"

"She's your *big* sister?"

"Yeah, she's twenty-seven. I'm just a babe of twenty-five." He gave her a wide grin.

"I hardly know Angelina. I've only spoken to her a few times."

Aside from seeing her lip-locked with Zach, which caused me to screw up my race.

"Angie's all right," Harper said. "Just kind of a girly-girl, you know. And she's a bit spoiled. She was the firstborn, and a girl, so Pa gave her whatever she wanted."

"I see. What happened between her and Zach?"

"Just differences. Was our families more than anything that pushed them together."

Dusty nodded, moved to the back of the stall, and stroked Regina's silky ears and kissed her velvety nose. Soft and sleek—she loved how Regina's ears felt under her fingers. Looking into her horse's big brown eyes, she tried to make her understand what she was about to do.

"You promise your baby sister will take good care of her?" A tear fell down Dusty's cheek.

"Yeah. I promise." Harper walked toward Dusty and wiped away the tear.

Dusty jerked backward. It didn't feel right for him to touch her.

"I'm sorry," Harper said.

"It's okay." She sniffed and held out her hand. "We've got a deal, Harper. Seventy-five thousand."

He clasped her hand and shook it in a tight grip. When he didn't let go, she pulled away forcefully.

Then she turned and walked out of the stall.

★ ★ ★

How she ended up at Diablo's pen, Dusty wasn't sure. She sat down, her back supported by a bale of hay, while the bull scruffed and snorted inside. She was alone. Everyone else was at the stock show or the rodeo. The practice rings were deserted but for a few ranch hands here and there. Just as well.

He had said he'd be her loudest cheerer. What a crock. Someone should have clued him in to the fact that it was impossible to cheer for the woman who had shared your bed when there was another woman's tongue stuffed down your throat.

Did it have to be during her race? Couldn't he have at least pretended to care?

She looked up at Diablo. The bull was staring at her calmly. She had the strangest feeling that Diablo knew she was sad, that he wanted to help her.

Zach might prefer sweet Mary Ann to her, but she could at least get her paws on his half mil purse. It was even more important now. Since that damned phone call...

With half a mil she could buy back Regina as well.

She rose and searched the bull's body. The flank strap was in place and looked about right—not too tight. Later, she'd berate Zach for leaving the strap on the animal while he was resting, but for now, he was ready to ride.

She looked Diablo in the eye. "It's just you and me, big boy," she said sweetly. "Just you and me. No one else is here. Nobody's going to hurt you."

She began to sing her Irish lullaby, this time reaching for the bull's flank and gently running her hands over his soft pelt. She walked around the pen, continuing to sing, and then reached his head and looked straight into his eyes. The animal was relaxed. It was time. She unlatched the gate and entered the pen.

Diablo didn't flinch as Dusty approached him. She latched the gate so she was locked in with him and moved to stand beside him, continuing to sing. After about ten minutes, she climbed up on a hay bale to mount him. And the most amazing thing happened.

He laid his body down in the soft dirt.

Dusty clasped her hand over her mouth, and tears welled in her eyes. He trusted her. He lay down so she could mount him. What a sweet, sweet animal.

She continued to croon to him as she lifted one leg over his large body and sat down gently, resisting her own weight at first and then adding it little by little until her full weight was on Diablo's back. She sat there for a few minutes, letting him get used to the feel of her, and then she leaned forward slowly, pressing her chest and then her cheek into his soft, bristly fur.

Oh, she was nervous, but she calmed herself, understanding that Diablo would draw from her emotions and her body language.

"What a sweet boy you are," she crooned, gently nudging her cheek into him.

She remained calm when she saw a pair of denim-clad legs walk toward the pen. She didn't know whose, but she was pretty sure they didn't belong to Zach. She knew his walk and his legs fairly well now.

"Shh," she said softly. "Don't frighten him." Her cheek was still nestled in the bull's back.

"Well, I'll be damned," the man said, nearly whispering. "I've never seen such a thing. That's a killer bull, Dusty."

Okay, this person knew her. "He's no killer. Just a misunderstood animal. He's sweet and gentle." She edged her gaze upward to the face of the stranger.

Harper Bay.

"Don't come any closer," Dusty whispered.

"I won't."

"I'm glad you're here. I'm going to try to get him to stand up. When I'm ready, I want you to open the gate."

"You're going to ride him?" Harper's voice was a little louder than Dusty was comfortable with, but Diablo didn't react.

"Shh," she said again. "Yes, but only if he's ready. He may not be. And that's okay. He'll let me eventually."

"But you don't have any gear on."

"It's okay."

"No, it's not. You're crazy. You at least need a glove. How are you going to hold the rope?"

"I'll be fine."

"Here." Harper strode toward her hesitantly, holding out a leather work glove. "It's not the best but it'll at least keep you from cutting your pretty hand."

"Slowly, Harper," Dusty warned.

He obeyed, and she took the glove. He was right. She did need it.

"You don't have chaps. Or a helmet."

"I'm fine."

"Damn, Dusty, I don't want to see you get hurt."

"He won't hurt me."

"He hurt Chad McCray pretty badly a year ago."

"I'm not Chad McCray."

"No, you're not." Harper kept his voice low and melodic, despite what he was saying. "That's my point."

"Shh." The soft whisper of her quieting command seemed to relax Diablo. "I'm going to sit up now and try to get him to stand."

"Dusty."

"Shh." She slowly lifted her body until she was sitting perpendicular to the bull. She willed her pulse to stay steady as she sat for a few moments. Then she gently squeezed her thighs together, and Diablo stood.

"I'll be goddamned," Harper said under his breath. "This is impossible. Damned impossible."

"No, it's not. You're witnessing it. How's his strap look?"

"Looks fine to me, but—"

"No buts." She stroked the bull's back. "Give me a few minutes. Then I want you to open the gate."

"No."

"Please, Harper."

"I can't."

"Please. I need this."

"Dusty..."

"Does your watch have a second hand?"

"Yeah."

"You're my timer. Zach will trust you if you say I rode him longer than eight seconds."

"So you've done this before?"

"Of course." Her voice was tranquil and harmonious. "Many times. Just not with this bull."

"Oh, God."

"It'll be all right." Dusty quietly toyed with Diablo's braided rope, tightly fastening it to her right hand. She was vaguely aware of more onlookers surrounding the practice ring, speaking in hushed voices. "That's a good boy. Such a good, big boy." She looked at Harper. "I'm ready. Unlatch the gate, and then get outside the ring. As soon as I tug on his rope he'll get mad, but I can handle him, I promise."

"Good Lord..."

"And don't forget to check the time on your watch as you unlatch."

Dusty shut her eyes and tried to reach Diablo mentally as she heard Harper unlatch the gate and swing it open. In a flash, Dusty opened her eyes and gave Diablo's rope a good yank. The bull bounded out into the ring, bucking and spinning.

So far, so good. Dusty could handle this. She continued talking to Diablo, hoping her voice would gentle him. Diablo knew his role well. He twisted. He spun. He bucked. He reared. Dusty felt every jolt, every ripple of his strong muscle. She reacted, matching him move for move, trying to make herself an extension of him and not a foreign object.

God, this animal was strong.

Come on, boy, she thought, trying to reach him mentally, emotionally. *We can do this. Yes, we can do this.*

She found his rhythm. She had reached him. What an adrenaline rush! She concentrated, holding him with her thighs, grasping the rope in her gloved hand. Yes, it was good. They were together. Completely.

But Diablo whisked away from her in a millisecond with a tremendous jerk. Caught off guard, Dusty flew through the air and stopped, her head striking the hard dirt of the ring.

She lifted her head, her vision cloudy, and attempted to move. Diablo stood several feet away from her, snorting and shuffling his hoof on the ground. The spell had broken. He no longer recognized her. Something had forced them apart, and he was coming for her. God, he was coming for her, but she couldn't move. *She couldn't move.*

Out of nowhere, a figure jumped into the ring. "Get her the hell out of here, Bay!"

Zach's voice. Zach was circling the bull.

Blackness fell as she fainted.

CHAPTER NINE

Dusty awoke in Harper Bay's arms.

"Shh," he said. "Don't try to talk. We've called 9-1-1, and one of the rodeo docs is on his way."

9-1-1? That was silly. She was fine. She opened her mouth to voice this thought, but nothing came out.

"Can you understand me, Dusty?" Harper asked.

Again, no words would come. She tried to nod her head, but wasn't sure if she was successful.

"I think she has a concussion." Harper's voice sounded distant, muffled.

"Let me take a look." Another voice.

Then a blinding light in her eye. "Pupils are responding. That's good. What was she doing on that bull, anyway?"

"Don't know."

Dusty tried to speak again, but failed.

"Well, she looks better than the other fella."

"How's he doing?"

"Gored pretty good in his thigh. He won't be bronc busting for a while."

Zach? Were they talking about Zach?

"But he's okay, right?"

"Yeah, he'll live. I cleaned him up as good as I could and sedated him, but he needs to go to the hospital for stitches and antibiotics. I'd like this little lady to go as well."

No. No hospitals. Hospitals held only pain and death.

Dusty opened her mouth to protest, but only a croak came out.

Please, not the hospital. Zach, I want Zach.

She drifted back into oblivion.

★ ★ ★

Dusty was dying of thirst. Her throat was parched. An iced tea would be heavenly. "Water?" she croaked.

Harper came to her quickly.

"Where am I?" she asked, her voice hoarse and raspy.

"The hospital, honey. You have a concussion."

She looked down and was dressed in a horrid hospital gown. Lying in a hospital bed.

Her worst nightmare.

No IV, though. Thank God.

"Zach?"

"He's here. He's going to be fine."

Thank God, thank God. "I don't want to see him."

"You don't have to see anyone you don't want to."

She tried to sit up, but realized quickly what a bad idea it was.

"I don't think so," Harper said, gently pushing her back down.

"I need to call my brother."

"I'll call him." He whipped out a cell phone. "What's the number?"

No cell phone. "Just leave a message for him. We're staying at the Holiday Inn downtown."

"I'll take care of it, honey. You just rest." He brought her a glass of ice chips. "Here, suck on these. It'll help."

Ice chips. To Dusty, the sweet water trickling down her

aching throat was nectar of the gods.

"Harper?"

"Yeah?"

"How long did I stay on?"

He chuckled softly. "Trust you to think of that right now."

"Well?"

"You were awesome. You stayed on for six seconds."

She closed her eyes. Not long enough. If she could only have made it for two more seconds...

Another failure.

She slept.

★ ★ ★

Runny scrambled eggs and a freaking knife in his thigh. Not Zach's ideal breakfast. The coffee sucked, too. Spending the night in the hospital during the stock show and rodeo was not on his agenda for these two weeks. All because of one stubborn, beautiful woman. He was madder than old Diablo himself. Thank God she was all right, though. He'd gotten a positive report from his morning nurse.

"Never fear, coffee's here!" Chad bellowed in his deep voice as he walked through the door, carrying two large Starbucks cups and an Einstein Bros Bagels bag. "Couldn't abandon you to hospital food, brother."

"You're a goddamned saint, Chad," Zach said, pushing his tray away. "Bring that stuff here. *Please.*"

"How are you feeling?"

"Been better." Zach took a long slow drink of coffee.

"I called Ma. She's on her way."

"Hell, she doesn't need to come out here for this."

"She was going to come tomorrow, anyway, for your bronc busting. Guess we can count that out now, huh?"

Zach sighed. "I guess you'll be the only one bringing home prize money this year, little brother."

"Yeah, I guess so. I'm real sorry this happened, Zach."

"Don't be."

"What was the twerp thinking?"

"Don't know." Zach winced as he shifted, his leg burning. "She had just screwed up her barrel race."

"Yeah, I saw it. Damn shame. She looked good. Real good."

"She sure did. What I saw of it, anyway."

"You weren't watching?"

"I was, but Angelina wouldn't leave me alone. She kept cackling in my ear like a goddamned prairie chicken. Then she..."

"She what?"

"She kissed me."

Chad's jaw dropped. "Whoa."

"You're telling me. I don't know what the hell she wants. *She* broke up with *me*. Not that I cared all that much. I feel like a heel for missing Dusty's race."

"Damn, bro, you're really whipped aren't you?"

Zach's heart lurched, but he forced his face into what he hoped was a nonchalant expression. Him? Whipped? "I wouldn't say that."

Chad chuckled. "I would."

"If only I understood her. Something's bothering her, I just know it. And this whole thing with Diablo. Why in the hell is she so obsessed with that bull?"

"It might have something to do with the half mil purse you've got on his head," Harper Bay said, entering the room.

"Morning, Zach. How are you feeling?"

"Like shit."

Harper grinned. "If it's any consolation, you look like shit too."

Zach ignored the insult and took a deep breath. "I've got a score to settle with you for letting the fool girl get on that bull, but that'll have to wait. What were you saying about the half mil purse?"

"Look, I tried to stop her, but—"

"Later, damn it. What about the purse?"

Harper cleared his throat. "I think she needs money."

Zach took a deep breath. He'd been thinking the same thing. Sharing a Holiday Inn room with her brother, no cell phone. "What makes you say that?"

"Just a hunch. That and the fact she sold me her barrel racing mare yesterday."

Zach nearly jumped out of his bed, the jolt sending a sharp pain through his wound. "Damn. That hurt."

"You need to simmer down, Zach," Chad said. "You're supposed to be taking it easy. You'd better cooperate if you want to get out of here this afternoon."

"She sold you her mare?"

"Yeah. I talked with her after her race. Told her I was looking to buy a horse for Catie, and hers was the best I'd seen. Drove a hard bargain, too. She wouldn't let the mare go until I offered seventy-five K."

Zach shook his head. "Dusty loves animals. I can't believe she'd sell one of her own."

"Like I said"—Harper sat down in a chair by the bed—"I think she needs the money."

"I need to see her," Zach said. "Help me out of the damn

bed, Chad."

"See her?" Chad shook his head. "You're not mad at her?"

"Are you crazy? I'm mad as shit. But something's going on, and I want to see her."

Chad's gaze drifted to Zach's bandage. "You can't put weight on that leg."

"Then I'll fucking hop, damn it." He grimaced as a dart shot through his thigh. "Now get over here and help me."

"Zach..." Harper cleared his throat.

"What?"

"I think I should tell you. She doesn't want to see you."

"Excuse me?"

"I was just with her. She's doing well." Harper hedged and cracked his knuckles. "She'll be leaving later today."

"What the hell were you doing with her?" Zach demanded.

"Just visiting. Her brother's with her now."

"Well, I'm going to see her."

"I think it would be best—" Harper began.

"I don't give a bloody damn what you think, Bay. I want to see my woman!"

"Your woman?"

Zach winced. His woman? Where had that come from? He was mad at the little fool. Still, the words echoed through to his soul. *His woman.* "Yeah. You got a problem with that?"

"No." Harper shook his head. "It's just that she led me to believe she was available, that's all."

Zach tensed. Harper was interested in Dusty. He could smell it. He felt like a wolf, fierce and possessive, with another male sniffing around his mate. The thought of Harper's hands on his woman made him want to throttle the guy.

"She's not." His voice was low, feral.

"All right. Jesus." Harper rose from his chair. "I think it's only fair to tell you, though, especially if you're involved with someone else. Angie thinks she's gonna start things up with you again."

"She made her intentions clear at your party. I told her I'm not interested."

"Good enough," Harper said. "For me, that is. But Angie's used to getting what she wants, and what she wants right now is you."

"She can't have me."

"I understand. Just don't expect her to accept no for an answer." Harper walked out the door, but turned his head and looked back. "Honestly, I'm glad you're okay, Zach."

"What are you standing there for?" Zach said to Chad. "I told you. I want to see my woman."

"Your woman is the reason you're in that hospital bed, Zach."

"I don't care. She's mine, and I want to see her."

Chad rolled his eyes. "I never thought I'd see the day. Fine. But don't you dare get up. I'll go get you a wheelchair."

Chad had no sooner left the room when Angelina trotted in, followed by Dallas and Chelsea. "Oh, God," Zach said under his breath.

"You poor thing," she gushed. "I came as soon as I could. How are you feeling?"

"Like shit."

She sat down on the edge of the bed and pushed his hair out of his eyes. He flinched.

"What can I do for you, sweetie pie?"

"Nothing. Chad's here, and my ma's on her way. I don't need anyone else fawning over me."

"Surely there's something I can do."

"Nothing." Zach sipped his coffee, which was now lukewarm.

"Now, Zach, Angie's just trying to help," Chelsea said.

"And I don't need her help, Chelsea."

"Honey, why don't you and Angie wait outside for a minute," Dallas said. "I want to talk to my brother alone."

"Christ," Zach said, as the women left. "What is it?"

"Are you going to believe me now?"

"About what? Dusty being no good for me?" Yes, the woman had gotten herself and him injured, and yes, he was mad, but no way in hell would he clue Dallas in on that fact. "No, I'm not."

"She got on your bull without permission. She could have been seriously hurt, and she would have sued us, and—"

"First of all, she's okay, thank God," Zach said. "And secondly, she wouldn't have sued us. She doesn't have a malicious bone in her body."

"She needs money, Zach."

"So? Who doesn't?"

"You don't, for one, and she knows it."

"If she wanted my money, she wouldn't be sneaking off with my bull." Zach shifted, and winced. "She'd be trying to trap me into marriage, like Chelsea did to you."

Dallas's mouth thinned into a grim line. "That's hitting below the belt, little brother. Chelsea didn't trap me. I wanted to marry her."

"You know as well as I do the Beaumonts were in financial trouble. Chelsea didn't want to give up her heiress ways, so she married money. You."

"We were in love."

"Were? Past tense, Dallas?"

"Are. I meant are." Dallas fidgeted with his Rolex.

Zach knew he'd hit a nerve. "Right. Whatever. Dusty is nothing like Chelsea." He spied Chad in the doorway with a wheelchair. "Chad's taking me on an...errand."

"I'll be here when you get back."

"Please, don't be." He grimaced as Chad helped him into the chair. Zach didn't look back as Chad wheeled him out of the room, IV rack in tow.

★ ★ ★

"This coffee is awful," Chelsea said, wrinkling her nose.

"I know. I hate hospitals. They're full of...sick people." Angelina examined her manicured nails.

"Right now this one is full of the man you want as your husband," Chelsea said, "so you'd better get used to being here."

"I know, I know." Angelina sighed. "This is turning out to be a more difficult project than I had anticipated. With that little trashy cowgirl hanging around him. And now she's put him in the hospital."

"It's too bad your little trick didn't work."

"You're telling me. That stupid flare gun recoiled and gave me a nasty charley horse in my arm."

"You didn't spook the bull?"

"I spooked him all right. And she landed on her butt and just sat there crying. I was afraid she'd really been hurt, and I freaked out a little. I never wanted to hurt her."

Chelsea scoffed. "Why not?"

Angelina looked at her friend's perfectly made-up face and saw something she wasn't sure she liked. Did Chelsea really want to see Dusty hurt? The little cowgirl was trashy, sure, but she didn't deserve that. "I didn't stick around to see what happened, but she raced today, so obviously she was fine."

"It didn't keep her away from the bull then."

"No, and consequently, it didn't keep her away from Zach."

"Well...you and Zach have a history. Can't you seduce him?"

"Tried it. I kissed him during the barrel race. I thought he was going to respond at first, but he pushed me away. Said he was sorry, but it was over."

"Hmm." Chelsea raised her perfectly plucked brows. "How was he in bed?"

"What does that have to do with anything?"

"Nothing." Chelsea grinned, her lined lips curving upward. "I'm just curious."

"He was great, actually. I always thought things were good between us. How's Dallas?"

"He's a cowboy, like Zach."

Angelina didn't push, although Chelsea was obviously evading the question. One only had to look at Dallas to know he was a stud in bed. He was as good looking as Zach, only more rugged. If only he weren't married—

She stopped that thought abruptly. Chelsea was her friend, after all. She cleared her throat. "So what can I do now?"

"What about Harper? He seems interested in her."

"Are you kidding me?"

"He couldn't keep his eyes off of her at your party. Didn't you notice?"

"Not really."

"And he was with her when she rode the bull today. If you get him interested in her..."

"You want me to sell out my baby brother for a man?"

"Well"—Chelsea's mouth curled into a smirk—"sometimes, when the stakes are high, one has to up the ante a little."

"But Harper?" Angelina shook her head. She had been willing to spook a bull, but sacrifice her brother to some low-class rancher girl? Of course, Chelsea *did* have a point about the stakes. She wanted Zach McCray. And Harper could charm the pants off just about anyone.

"Exactly what do you have in mind?"

Chelsea winked at her. "Come on. Let's go shopping. There's a sale on shoes at Nordstrom."

"And?"

"And my mind is always at its best when I'm trying on shoes."

★ ★ ★

Dusty lay on her hospital bed. "I don't want to see him."

"I understand," Harper said, standing next to the chair where Sam sat. "I just thought I should let you know he seemed downright determined to see you."

"What's the problem, Dust?" Sam asked. "You do owe him an explanation, don't you think? You hijacked his bull and put him in the hospital."

"I was perfectly fine. He didn't need to come charging in like a knight in shining armor. I wasn't some damsel in distress. I had Diablo under control."

Sam clenched his fists together. "I still can't believe you let her get on that bull, Bay."

"She was on the bull by the time I got there. It would have

been more dangerous for me to interfere."

"You didn't have to unlatch the gate."

"I know."

Dusty recognized the anger in Sam's eyes, but none of this was Harper's fault. "I made him, Sam."

"Right. You had a gun to his head."

"Your brother's right, Dusty," Harper said. "I never should have unlatched the gate. But—"

"No buts," Sam said.

"You're right. It was just something in her voice."

"You're both nuts," Sam said.

"He's right," Dusty said. "About me needing to be with Diablo."

"Whatever."

"Hey," Harper said, "I just came by to warn you that McCray's on his way. I'm glad you're feeling better, Dusty. Hope to see you out on the grounds soon."

"I'll be there tomorrow."

"No, you won't, young lady," Sam said, his tone parental.

"Why not? I'm perfectly fine."

"You're recovering from a concussion." Her brother shook his head. "If I have to get the doctor to tie you down, I will."

Dusty huffed. Sam was right, of course. There'd be no more competing, either. She'd blown it big time. No winnings, and she had lost Regina. And there was the problem of that phone call, which she hadn't told Sam about yet. "Fine."

"Now you're talkin' some sense," came a voice from the doorway. Zach wheeled himself into the room with one arm, dragging his IV stand with the other.

He had an IV. Dusty's heart collapsed, and she looked away, concentrating on the figures of Harper and Sam.

"If you'll excuse us, Harper, Sam, I'd like to speak to Dusty."

"That's up to her, I think," Harper said.

"Damn it, Bay—"

Sam grabbed Harper's shoulder and ushered him out. "You're entitled to a few minutes, Zach," he said, "but don't upset her."

"The last thing I want is to see her upset." Zach wheeled himself over to Dusty's head. Once Chad had shut the door, Zach leaned over and kissed Dusty's forehead. "Thank God you're all right."

Dusty's throat tensed. He was going to be nice to her. It would be so much easier if he were angry. He had a right to be. As upset as she was with him, she hadn't had the right to ride Diablo without his permission.

"I'm sorry," she said meekly.

"I know."

"Why aren't you mad?"

He chuckled. "I *am* mad. My thigh hurts like a mother, I can't compete, and someone I care about is hurt due to her own stupidity."

"Hey—"

"Sorry, darlin', but getting on Diablo all by yourself like that was stupid, and you know it. Even I can't believe it, but I'm just so relieved you're not seriously injured."

Dusty gulped, tears forming in her eyes. Why did he have to look so wonderful? His hair was tousled and sexy, his face unshaven and rugged, and he wore green flannel pajama pants and a silk robe. She was still furious with him, yet she burned for him. Her entire body trembled at his nearness.

"It'll be okay," Zach said.

"No." She sniffed. "Nothing's okay."

"I'll make it okay. I swear it."

"You can't."

"I can. I want to. If you'll just tell me—"

"No!" Dusty's pulse quickened. "I-I'm glad you're okay, Zach. I never wanted you to get hurt. But you can't help me. Just go away. I don't want you here."

"Damn it, Dusty. Why won't you let me in?"

Let him in? Oh, that was a good one. "I did. I did let you in. I let you into my body."

"I'm not talking about your body."

"I am. I gave you something I'd never given anyone, something that was mine to give only one time. I did it gladly. I wanted it. But you...you... Oh!" She turned over, away from him.

Within seconds, he had wheeled himself to the other side of the bed. "Darlin', what is it? Do you need money?"

How humiliating. "You think this is about money? You're infuriating!"

"Dusty—"

She clenched her fists. "I lost the barrel race because of you!"

"Me?"

"I lost my horse. I can't rope tomorrow. And I only stayed on Diablo for six seconds. Six seconds, Zach! That's three seconds longer than you've been able to ride him. But it's still two seconds short, isn't it? So I don't get the purse, do I?"

"If you need the money, I'll gladly give you the purse."

"You will, huh? A cool half mil. Is that what a twenty-three-year-old virgin is worth these days? Makes me a damned expensive whore, doesn't it?"

God, she had gone too far. His blue eye darkened, and his brown eye smoked. Anger. Raw, crazy wrath. Well, let him be angry then. He should be. She had gotten him hurt. She was no stranger to anger, herself. She was damned mad at him. Damned mad at the whole world.

"You're so determined to push me away." His voice cracked. "Fine, I can take a hint." His hands clamped onto the wheels of his chair, his knuckles white with tension.

"Don't you get all high and mighty with me," she said. "I'm not the one who was making out with Angelina yesterday. That was you. And during my race!"

His eyes softened. "You saw that?"

"Yeah, I saw that, and I lost because of it."

"Oh, God, darlin'."

"Don't call me that. It's nothing but a lie. Now get out."

"But if you'll let me explain—"

Sam opened the door and walked in. "You need to leave now, Zach. She's all upset."

"I'm not done talking with her."

"Yeah, you are. For now. Go on."

When Zach looked back at her, Dusty looked away. He didn't argue any more with Sam. "I'll come by to see her later."

"Maybe not a good idea. There'll be plenty of time for you all to talk when you're both in better condition."

"All right." The door closed with a gentle whoosh, and Zach was gone.

Her mattress sank as Sam sat down next to her. "I'm sorry, Dust."

She sniffed. "No matter."

"What is this really about?" He took her hand.

For a moment, Dusty flashed back seventeen years, to the

day their father had told them about their mother's terminal condition. Sam had grabbed her small hand and rubbed her palm with his thumb, like he was doing now. His thumb was callused now. She swallowed hard.

"Is it the money?" Sam said. "Because if it is, stop worrying about it. That old ranch isn't worth it. We'll be fine."

Dusty swallowed. The time had come to tell him. "The ranch may not be worth it, Sam. But my life is. The hospital called yesterday. My white cell count is up."

HELEN HARDT

CHAPTER TEN

"God, Sis, I'm so sorry." Sam's grip on her hand tightened.

"They want me back in three weeks for a recheck."

"That's good."

Dusty let out a breathy scoff. "How exactly is that good?"

"If they were overly concerned, they'd get you back in right away." Sam loosened his grip, but tension shone on his face. "It could be something as harmless as your immune system fighting off a cold."

"Yeah, that's what they said."

"So we'll think positive until we know more."

"Easy for you to say." Dusty sighed. "So close to my five-year mark, and now this." The trickle of a tear tickled her cheek, and she wiped it away. "Plus, the bill for this stupid hospital stay, which is totally my fault, I know."

"It won't be much. A couple thousand..."

"A couple thousand that could have gone toward the ranch. But no worries. I can pay the bill."

"How? You didn't win the barrel race."

"Regina. I sold Regina to Harper Bay."

"Dust..."

"I didn't have a choice. We need the money, and I blew the barrel race. If I need more treatment—"

"You'll get the treatment you need, if I have to work five goddamned jobs. We haven't come this far to lose the battle now."

"I don't want you working like a dog, Sam."

"It's the least I can do. I'd take the treatment for you if I could, but since that's not an option, I'll at least see that we can pay for it."

Dusty reached for her brother, and he took her in his arms.

"It's going to be okay," he said. "I'll take care of you."

"You shouldn't have to take care of me. You're twenty-seven. You should be settling down, raising a family. Not burdened with a sick sister and a bankrupt ranch."

"You're not a burden."

An anvil settled in Dusty's stomach. "I sure feel like one."

"You aren't. You never were."

She turned from her brother's gaze. "Papa thought so."

"No, he didn't. What Papa did had nothing to do with you."

"It was because of me he needed money."

"But it wasn't your fault. You didn't ask to get sick."

She sighed. "That's the truth of it."

"I do have some good news. Your doctor signed your release papers. Can you get dressed by yourself, or do you need help?"

"I can do it."

"Good. I'm going down to the billing office to take care of things."

"Tell them we'll send the money within the month. Harper will probably pay me in the next few days for Regina."

"Will do. I'll be back in a few."

Dusty felt a little lightheaded when she rose from the bed, but it passed. She changed out of the dreaded hospital gown and into the clean jeans and shirt Sam had brought for her, and she sat back down on the bed and waited for him.

Within about fifteen minutes he returned.

"I take it everything went okay?" Dusty said.

"Yes. In fact, it did." Sam sat down in the chair next to the bed.

"Good."

"Dusty, what's going on between you and Zach McCray?"

His name made her heart thump. "Nothing."

"That night you didn't come home. You were with him, weren't you?"

"That's not really any of your business, Sam."

"I know you're over eighteen and all. I can't pretend I'm comfortable with my baby sister doing...*that*, but you certainly have the right. But I need to know. Were you with him?"

Dusty sighed and nodded slowly.

"Okay."

"Why? Why are you asking about that now?"

"Well"—he cleared his throat—"it seems your hospital bill has been paid in full. By Zach McCray."

★ ★ ★

Dusty took a deep breath and knocked on the door to Suite 2500 of the Windsor Hotel. After a good night's sleep in her own hotel room, she was feeling almost like herself, and she needed to speak to Zach about paying her medical bill. When the door opened, she looked straight into the emerald-green eyes of Angelina Bay.

"Hello, Angelina. I need to speak with Zach."

"Dusty, you're just the person I want to see." Angelina grabbed her arm and pulled her into the suite. "I'm so glad to see you up and around."

"You are?" Angelina was being nice to her, and using her

actual name? Something was definitely up.

"Of course. I was so upset to hear about your accident with the bull. Harper has talked of nothing else. He's been so worried about you."

"He has?" Dusty wrinkled her brow.

"Yes, he talks of nothing but you. You've certainly made quite an impression on him."

"Uh..." Dusty searched for words. Angelina was up to something for sure, but Dusty wanted only to see Zach. She'd deal with Mary Ann later.

"You should be proud. Women have been chasing him for years. Who would have thought a cute little cowgirl from Montana would be the one to steal his heart?"

"Angelina, I have no idea what you're talking about. I hardly know Harper. He and I have a business relationship. He bought my horse."

"For Catie. Yes, I know. She's going to love you, and I know you'll be an excellent influence on her. You can teach her all you know about barrel racing."

"Exactly how will I teach her from Montana?"

"You silly! I mean after you and Harper are married, of course."

Dusty's mouth dropped. "Excuse me?"

"I didn't stammer, did I?"

"I'm not sure what Harper has told you, but we're not getting married. We're not dating. We've hardly had a conversation. Now if you don't mind, I need to see Zach."

"I suppose I've put the cart before the horse." Angelina smiled. "I tend to do that. I just know you're the one to tame my brother, though. There's something in his eyes when he talks about you."

"Truly, I don't know what you're talking about. Now about Zach."

Angelina compressed her lips into a thin line. "He's asleep."

Dusty walked past her. "I'll wait if you don't mind."

"Actually, under the circumstances, I think—"

"Who is it, Angie?" came another female voice.

Dusty turned to see Zach's mother, Laurie McCray. She was still tall and beautiful, her sleek black hair now salted with silver and cut into a stylish wedge.

"Dusty O'Donovan." Laurie smiled, the laugh lines around her eyes adding character to her lovely face. "I couldn't believe it when Zach and Chad told me you and your brother were here. Last time I saw you, you were knee high to a grasshopper. What a gorgeous woman you've become."

The woman embraced Dusty and rubbed her back. Dusty trembled slightly.

"What's the matter, sugar?" Laurie asked.

"It's wonderful to see you again," Dusty said. "I-I just want you to know. I never would have intentionally hurt Zach. I know this is all my fault."

"Don't be silly." Laurie squeezed Dusty's arm gently. "Zach doesn't blame you, and neither do I. In fact, I'm quite impressed. He says you stayed on his bull for six seconds."

"Yes, I did. But that's not important right now. How is Zach?"

"He's fine. Nothing keeps that boy down. He's a little sleepy, but he's going to be just fine."

"I'd like to talk to him, if possible."

"I'm sure he'd love to see you."

"Actually," Angelina said, "I just told Dusty he was asleep."

"No, he's awake," Laurie said. "You go on in, sugar. Angie and I'll stay here in the living room and give you all some privacy."

"Are you sure this is a good idea, Laurie?" Angelina asked. "He shouldn't be upset."

"This sweet thing won't upset him."

"I'm not so sure," Dusty heard Angelina say under her breath.

"What?" Laurie asked.

"Nothing." Angelina sat down on the sofa. "By all means, go on in."

Zach was lying on his bed when Dusty entered the bedroom. On top of the covers, his chest bare, his legs clad in plaid lounging pants. He still hadn't shaved, but his hair had been combed back over his forehead. Dusty wanted to thread her fingers through it and let it fall in soft waves around his face.

"Hey, darlin'," he said.

"Hey yourself."

"I thought I heard your voice."

She nodded. "How are you?"

"Better, now that you're here."

She warmed, and imagined rosiness creeping up her neck. Why was he always so sweet to her? "I need to talk to you."

"Talk away."

She cleared her throat and sat down on the edge of the bed. "About my hospital bill—"

"I know what you're going to say. But I wanted to help. I want to be there for you. I want to be *with* you."

"What about Angelina?"

"I tried to explain that yesterday, but you wouldn't let me.

There is no Angelina."

"You kissed her."

"She kissed *me*. Not the other way around. Inopportune timing, I admit. I'm so sorry about your race. And I told her I wasn't interested."

"My losing the race wasn't your fault, Zach." Dusty feathered her fingers over his cheek. "I shouldn't have yelled at you about it."

"You were upset."

"Yeah. But it was still my fault. I was in control, not you. I shouldn't have let anything break my concentration."

"Why'd you look up?"

"I always do, around the third barrel. Seeing the crowd cheering always gives me a rush to finish. I just didn't expect to see you kissing Angelina."

"I know. I'm sorry."

"She wants to get back together with you?"

"Evidently."

Dusty rolled her eyes. "Well, that explains a few things."

"Like what?"

"The sales pitch she just gave me."

"Huh?"

"She told me Harper is just nuts about me. She's probably trying to get me off your trail."

"No way. I want you on my trail." Zach's body tensed. "Harper can just stay the hell away from you."

"I don't think he's interested in me. We hardly know each other."

"Oh, he's interested. Who wouldn't be?"

Dusty broadened her smile. "Well, I'm not interested. In him, that is. He's a nice man and all, but..."

"But what?"

"Nothing." Suddenly she felt shy. "If you're not interested in starting things up with Angelina again, why is she here?"

"Because she's a damn stubborn fool."

"Can't you kick her out?"

"I've tried. But my ma's here, and she and Angie's ma are best friends. So I'm in a bit of a bind."

Dusty couldn't help the little smile that edged its way along her lips. "Be that as it may, I can't let you pay my bills, Zach."

"It's already done, darlin'."

"You'll just have to undo it."

"Why can't you let me do this for you? I only want to help."

"I know." Dusty threaded her fingers through his thick locks. "But this whole thing is my fault. I should be paying *your* bills."

"I'm insured." He grinned at her. "Don't stop," he said, when she took her hands from his hair. "It feels good."

"I don't want to owe you anything."

"You don't."

"I feel like...because of what we did, that you think you need to... I don't know... Do stuff for me."

"That's the silliest thing I ever heard."

"Good. Because I want you to know, I slept with you because I wanted to, not to get your money."

"You don't have to say any of this."

"I just don't want you to think—"

"I don't." He touched her cheek and ran his thumb over the tip of her nose. He curled his hand around the nape of her neck and pulled her toward him. "Come here."

"Zach, I don't know."

"Just a kiss. One kiss."

He brushed his mouth gently over hers. "You have the sweetest lips," he whispered. "Full and cherry red and delicious."

He nibbled across her upper lip and then her lower. She shuddered, the sensation filling every cell in her body. When his tongue probed for entrance, she granted it, moaning softly and responding. Her hand crept across his chest, and she laced her fingers through the dark curls and caressed the taut muscle underneath. His mouth tasted even sweeter than she remembered, and she explored more deeply, kissing him harder, faster.

They both finally broke away to breathe. Then he took her lips again.

"You said one kiss," she rasped against his chin.

"I lied." He thrust his tongue into her mouth again.

The pleasure, the sweet, sinful joining of mouths. She could kiss him forever, she was sure of it. She melted into him, sighed into his mouth softly, sucked and bit at his lips, his tongue.

"Zach?"

Angelina's voice. What a mood killer. Dusty broke the kiss and looked toward the door.

"Jesus, Angie," Zach said. "Can't you see we're busy in here?"

"You shouldn't be straining yourself."

"I'm not. I'm kissing my woman."

Dusty's heart leaped. *His woman.* It couldn't last, but oh, she loved the thought of it. She loved that he said it in front of Angelina.

"And if you'll excuse us," Zach continued, "I'd like to get

back to it."

"Well—"

"Go on. Go shopping or something. Take my mother with you. I'd like some privacy."

Angelina turned with a huff and shut the bedroom door behind her.

"Your mother, Zach, I don't want her to think—"

"I'm a grown man of thirty, darlin'. I don't give a flying fuck what my mother thinks. Now kiss me."

Dusty breathed, her pulse pounding. "Why do you do this to me? Why do I want you so much?"

"Because you're mine. You always have been. I think in some innocent childish way I knew it the first time I laid eyes on you."

He pulled her against his body and kissed her again, a deep kiss this time. A firm, relentless meeting of mouths. A kiss of possession. He was marking his territory. Marking her. She felt it all the way to the tips of her toes, and she liked it. She liked it very much.

He nibbled and licked at her face, her neck, her ears. "Come to bed with me," he said huskily. "I need you."

Dusty shook her head, her lips pressed to his neck. "No," she whispered. "You're weak. We both are. It's not a good idea."

"It's a great idea."

"Oh my God."

"You want me. I can feel how much you want me." His whispers were soft caresses against her cheek. "Please."

"Yes, I want you." How could she lie? He knew, anyway. She had never known such wanting, such desire, such incredible depth of feeling.

"Slide my pants over my hips, darlin'. Be careful of the

bandage."

"I don't want to hurt you."

"God, you won't. I promise you won't. Right now I feel like I'll die if I can't have you."

Dusty leaned down and circled her lips over one fleshy nipple, twirling her tongue in Zach's chest hair, as she slid her hands down his ribbed abdomen to his pajama bottoms. She felt him suck in a breath as her fingers slid under the waistband. She dived in farther with one hand, the hardness of his erection too great a temptation to resist. She touched it tentatively, and he groaned, jerking slightly.

"I'm so sorry. Did I hurt you?"

"God, no."

"I just wanted to touch you."

"You can touch any part of me." He chuckled softly. "Especially that part."

She gathered her courage and grasped his cock. He was so big and so hard, yet smooth. Smooth and velvety and perfectly formed. Magnificent.

"That's great, darlin', but it'll work better if we lose the pants."

"Oh." Dusty chewed on her lip and wiped her clammy hands on her jeans. "Right." The pants. That's what had started this in the first place. She gently eased the soft fabric over his hips and beheld his arousal springing from its black nest. Her sense of touch had been right—perfectly formed and magnificent.

"You're beautiful," she said.

"I'll take that as a compliment." He laughed.

"Oh, it is. It *so* is. I... I want to put my mouth on you."

He groaned. "Oh, God. Please."

"I think it's only fair to tell you," Dusty hedged, embarrassed. "I-I don't exactly know what I'm doing."

"It's okay. You'll be perfect. I know it."

Dusty nodded, and then pressed her lips gently to the head. A drop of clear liquid emerged, and she smeared it over the head with her thumb and licked it off.

Zach began panting. "Dusty. Go lock the bedroom door. Then take off your clothes."

CHAPTER ELEVEN

Zach McCray's cock was in her mouth. It was smooth. And hot. And salty. And delicious. And she was enjoying every minute of it. Judging from the moans coming from Zach, he was, too.

Such power. Such complete recklessness. She could get used to this.

"I want to taste you too," he rasped. "Come here." He pulled her to him and turned her around, positioning her over his head. "Sit here."

"Zach…"

"Sit here, darlin'. We can both have our fun."

His tongue found her and drove into her. She squirmed on him, too timid to push down with her weight. When he grabbed the cheeks of her bottom, spreading her, pulling her tightly against his face, she figured it would be okay to grind into him as she desired. She wasn't disappointed.

Between his legs, his cock beckoned. Yes, they could both have their fun. She leaned forward and took him into her mouth, and suddenly his assault on her became more urgent, more relentless. As she climaxed, she forced her mouth down upon him, taking as much as she could. He ripped his mouth from her, his breath coming in rapid puffs against her damp thighs.

"Come ride me. I need to be inside you."

Dusty crawled forward, turned, and positioned herself over his massive erection. Slowly she eased herself downward until she had completely sheathed him.

Oh, the sweet sensation of being filled to the brim. Of being stroked and caressed so perfectly.

"That's right," he said. "Move on me."

She slowly rode him, up and down, circling her hips so he touched every inch of her moist walls.

"You're so tight, darlin'. So sweet. Come here."

She leaned forward for his kiss, continuing her motion, wanting him deeper, harder. She thrust downward as he thrust upward, their bodies meeting, the slapping, sticky sounds of their lovemaking a sensual symphony to her ears.

She broke the kiss and sat straight up, taking his full length inside of her. She closed her eyes and cupped her breasts, sliding her nipples between her fingers and tugging on them.

"God, you're beautiful," Zach said. "I love to watch you touch yourself."

Dusty panted and breathed. "I wish it were your tongue on my nipples, Zach."

"Bring 'em here then."

She obliged, and he took a nipple between his teeth. The jolt from his attack went straight to her sex. She came with a startling vibration.

"Oh, yeah," Zach said, his mouth still pressed to her breast. "Ride me hard. I want to come with you."

She pounded on top of him, digging her fingernails into his chest.

"That's it, that's it," he groaned. "Damn. Damn, that's good." He thrust into her, and the spasms of his orgasm fluttered against her walls.

She fell forward into his arms. "Zach, Zach," she whispered.

"What?"

"Nothing." She lifted herself from him, the wetness between them making little suction noises. She nestled herself into the crook of his arm, and then remembered his wound. She rose into a sitting position and turned to look at the bandage.

"Are you all right?" she asked. "I didn't hurt you, did I?"

"Are you kidding? This is the best I've felt since the last time we did this. Damn, I've missed you."

"I missed you too. But shouldn't we take care of your bandage? Do you need it changed?"

"It'll be okay for a while. Come lie with me for a few minutes. Then we'll order some dinner."

"Zach, your mother and Angelina will be back soon. We should really get dressed and invite them to join us for dinner."

"I don't want to have dinner with them. I want to have dinner with my woman."

"Your woman."

"Yeah." His beautiful eyes twinkled. "I like the sound of that. I like that you're my woman."

"Zach..."

"Don't you want to be my woman, Dusty?"

More than she wanted to breathe, at that particular moment. But, "Zach?"

"Hmm?"

"Did you and Angelina...sleep together?"

He sighed into her hair. "What was between Angelina and me has nothing to do with us."

"Yeah, I know, and I also know it's a stupid question. I mean, you're thirty, and you were engaged to her."

"I haven't lived like a monk, darlin'."

Of course he hadn't. He was amazing. "I never thought

you had."

Zach took her hand and caressed it. "Dusty, let me be serious for a minute, okay?" His gaze darkened, and his tone lowered. "I've never made love lightly. I always had feelings for the woman. But I can tell you, honestly, that what I felt for Angelina isn't anything compared to how I feel about you."

"But you were engaged."

"So?"

"You made a commitment to her."

"It was a mistake."

"And she broke it off, not you."

"If she hadn't, I would've."

"What happened?"

"It's a long, boring story, Dusty. A story of two families and a lot of money and a lot of land, and I promise I'll tell you sometime, but right now, can we just be together and not talk about Angelina?"

Dusty smiled, lay down next to him, and buried her face in his shoulder. "I suppose so."

"You're the only woman I want." He entwined his fingers through her thick golden hair. "I love your hair. It's so beautiful. It's like silk in my hands."

Her hair.

What a shocking jolt back to reality. Her long, beautiful hair. Would he still love it when it was falling in clumps in the bathroom?

"I have to go, Zach. Sam is expecting me."

"Dusty, please don't run from me again. It's getting old."

"But—"

"Sam's a big boy. He can take care of himself. He and Chad are probably drinking beer and chasing women."

"I know." She sighed.

"Are you ever going to tell me what's going on with you?" Zach asked, still stroking her hair.

"There's nothing going on." She hid her face and inhaled. Even his armpits smelled good, like musk and cloves.

Zach nudged her and turned on his side, wincing. "Fuck."

"Don't move. Are you all right?"

"Yeah. Yeah." He tipped her chin upward to look into her eyes. "Look, I won't push you to talk, but if you're going to be with me, don't ever lie to me again."

"I'm not lying."

"Damn it, Dusty. I know there's something going on. If you're not ready to tell me, I can accept that. I don't like it, mainly because I want to move heaven and earth to help you, but I can accept it." His blue eye glowed the color of a hot gas flame. "But do not lie to me."

"All right, Zach. I won't lie to you. Just don't ask me anymore."

"Fair enough," he said. "Just know that whatever it is, it won't make a damn difference to me."

"How can you say that without knowing what it is?"

"Because I care about you, you damn stubborn woman!"

No. He couldn't care for her. He'd get hurt. "Zach, you hardly know me. We really only just met a few days ago."

"Don't try to tell me what I feel. I'm thirty years old, and I never say anything other than what I mean. I care for you. I want to be with you. I think it'll grow into something more. Something amazing."

"Zach, I don't know..."

"You don't have to say anything."

Dusty burst into tears.

Zach sighed. "Not exactly the reaction I'd hoped for."

"I'm sorry," she sobbed. She wanted to return his feelings. She wanted to profess her undying love and stay with him forever, but that wouldn't be fair to him. He deserved better than what she could offer him. "Just don't pressure me, okay?"

"I won't. I know you're not ready to talk to me yet, but when you are, I'll be here, and I'm not going anywhere."

"What did I ever do to deserve you?"

He chuckled. "You're so adorable. So damned perfect."

Perfect. Perfect she was not. If he only knew. But she didn't want to cry anymore. She wanted to share this night with Zach and pretend everything was all right, but it wasn't right to lead him on.

"I can't stay with you tonight, Zach."

"Yes, you can. You have to." His eyes smiled at her. "You're the reason I'm in this situation, darlin'. I need you to take care of me."

"I think your ma and Angelina can handle that."

"I don't want them. I want my woman to take care of me."

He sure knew how to get to her. She wanted to be his woman. She wanted to take care of him, and the territorial lioness in her didn't want Angelina anywhere near him. True enough—it was her fault he was wounded. She owed him her care. And it was a good excuse to spend the night with him, anyway.

"I'll stay," she said.

"Wonderful. Let's order up some dinner, and then I'll let you play nursemaid." He grinned rakishly. "You may have to bathe me."

"It would be my pleasure."

"Darlin', the pleasure will be mine."

★ ★ ★

Zach couldn't immerse his wound, so Dusty gave him a sponge bath after dinner. It was a pleasure to cleanse his strong body. She especially enjoyed washing his genitals, seeing his cock grow before her eyes as she fondled him. "This is a bath," she teased, "not foreplay."

When she finished bathing him, she helped him on crutches to the bathroom and shaved his face.

"Have you ever thought about growing a beard?"

"Not really. Why?"

"I like the feel of it when we kiss, and when you do...other things." She warmed.

"Then I'll grow a beard for you. But I'll have to start tomorrow, because you just shaved it off."

"A short goatee would look good on you. With your long hair, it would be a nice contrast. You'd look even more like a movie star than you already do."

"You think I look like a movie star?"

"The handsomest one in Hollywood." She rinsed his face with a warm cloth. "Now lower your head. I'm going to wash your beautiful hair."

When she finished, she changed the linens on the bed, which were damp from his sponge bath, and helped him get comfortable.

"Okay, soldier," she said. "Time to look at the wound. Tell me what to do."

"The dressing and antibiotic ointment are in the top dresser drawer," he said, motioning. "You'll need to clean it with peroxide first."

"Okay." She took a deep breath and removed the bandage

slowly, trying not to hurt him. She gasped when she saw his wound—several tight black stitches laced around a pinkish gash. "You poor thing. I'm so sorry!"

"I'm fine."

"Zach, it's all red, and it's swollen. It's oozing a little, too. It doesn't look right to me. I hope it's not infected."

"It's not deep," Zach said. "I didn't need surgery or anything. I've seen worse, believe me. Much worse. It's just a nick. They wouldn't have let me out of the hospital if it was bad."

"How can you still want to be with me after I did this to you?"

"You didn't do anything. It was Diablo, last time I checked."

"Still..."

"Darlin', you're my woman. I want you. Nothing will change that."

If only that were the case, Dusty thought. No matter. Right now Zach needed her, and she wasn't going to let him down. She saturated a cotton ball with peroxide and cleaned the wound. The solution bubbled as it touched the injury, and Zach tensed.

"Okay?" she asked.

"Yeah. Fine," he said through clenched teeth.

Once she felt it was clean enough, she smeared it with antibiotic ointment and covered it with gauze and a clean bandage.

"Do you have any pills you need to take? Pain pills? Antibiotics?"

"I took both of them with dinner."

"Okay. Anything else?"

"Just you in my arms. That's all I need."

She smiled. "I guess I can handle that." She shed the robe she wore and crawled into bed next to him. "No funny business. I want you to sleep. You need your rest."

"You take the fun out of everything." He yawned.

"See? You're exhausted."

"Mmm," he said. "Maybe a little sleep wouldn't hurt." He wrapped his arms around her. "As long as you're here when I wake up."

"I'm not going anywhere."

"Promise?"

"Yeah."

For now, anyway.

CHAPTER TWELVE

Heat. Blind heat. And trembling. Something was shaking next to her. Dusty woke from her dreams to find Zach clamped to her body. He was burning with fever.

She started to move, but he tightened his grip on her. "C-C-Cold," he said through clenched teeth. "D-Don't go."

"Zach, sweetheart, I have to get up. I have to take care of you. I think you have a fever."

"M-More covers," he said.

It killed her to leave him, knowing she was his source of warmth. She checked the clock on the night table. Two-thirty. "I'm sorry. I'll be back as soon as I can. I need to check your wound. I told you it didn't look right earlier. It must be infected."

"D-Don't leave me."

"I won't. I'll be right here."

She scrambled away from him and out of bed and pushed the sheets and blankets around his shivering body. She turned on the lights and blinked at the harsh invasion. "Zach," she said, "I have to look at your leg. I'm just going to get your leg out from under the covers, but I'll keep the rest of you tucked in, okay?"

He nodded his head, his teeth chattering.

Carefully Dusty pulled his leg out from under the blankets and deftly removed the bandage. She gasped as she gaped at the pus draining from the injury. Small pink lines radiated from the wound, marring his beautiful skin.

"Zach, I need to take you to the hospital. You have an infection."

He continued to shiver and didn't respond to her.

"Can you get up?"

He shook his head. "C-Can't. T-Too cold."

"You have to. Please. I'll help you." She pulled at him but realized she wouldn't be able to move him without help. She wished she could give him something for the fever, but she was afraid to mix anything over-the-counter with his prescriptions.

She reached for the phone on the night table and dialed the front desk. "I need some help. Mr. McCray has a fever, and I need to get him to the hospital."

"I'll call 9-1-1, ma'am."

"Thank you." Dusty shrugged. She could have done that herself. What was she thinking? She needed to get her head on straight. Her man needed her.

Her man.

Yes, her man. He was her man. He had been all along. There was no fighting it. In some sinless way, she had known since she was six, the last day she had seen him, when he had told her to keep her chin up. And she had. Through all the hard times and the pain, she had. She had learned what was worthy of her fear and what wasn't because of that lanky adolescent who had treated her with kindness.

She would never love another.

Quickly, she dressed herself and then helped Zach into his lounge pants. "Sweetheart," she said, "where's your cell phone?"

"D-Drawer."

"Which drawer?" When he didn't answer she began

opening and closing drawers frantically until she found it in with his underwear. She thumbed through his contact list and called Chad and his mother. Within minutes they were both in Zach's room.

"Let's get him down to the lobby," Chad said and scooped his brother into his arms. "You're a heavy SOB, aren't you?" Chad's face was somber when Zach didn't respond.

"He's cold," Dusty said. "Please, he needs blankets. Or at least a robe." She grabbed one of the white hotel robes and tucked it around Zach. Tears slid from her eyes. He looked so helpless in his brother's arms.

"Come now, sugar." Laurie McCray put her arms around Dusty. "I just thank God you were here with him. He's going to be all right."

They reached the lobby as the ambulance was pulling into the circular drive at the front. Two paramedics lifted Zach onto a stretcher, and one of them asked if anyone wanted to ride with him.

"I will." Dusty raced forward.

"You his wife?" the paramedic asked.

"Uh, no. I'm his...girlfriend."

"We prefer it to be a family member."

Laurie stepped forward. "I'll go. I'm his mother."

"Please," Dusty begged. "I need to be with him."

"Come on, twerp." Chad grabbed her hand. "You and I can follow in the pickup."

Dusty nodded through hiccups and tears.

Chad fished a bandana out of his pocket. "Here."

She took it and wiped her eyes. "Thanks."

"He's gonna be okay. The fool's too stubborn for something like this to keep him down."

Dusty nodded and sniffed again.

"And he doesn't blame you. He probably should, but he doesn't. But you're going to have to tell him the truth eventually."

"What do you mean?"

"I mean the truth. About you. About the ranch."

"How much has Sam told you?"

"Just that you're struggling. The ranch needs money."

She breathed a sigh of relief. Sam hadn't betrayed her trust. *Thank God.*

"I'm sure Zach has already guessed that much," she said.

"Undoubtedly." Chad nodded. "But it'll mean more to him if you tell him. Confide in him. He'll help you."

"Why on earth would he help me?"

"Because he's in love with you."

She looked up to Chad's face. "He told you that?"

"Hell, no. He didn't have to. It's obvious. I've never seen him ferocious over a woman before. That's the only word to describe his reaction when Harper indicated an interest in you."

"We've only just met."

"You just referred to yourself as his girlfriend. I heard you."

Chad opened the door to the pickup and Dusty scrambled inside. Chad sat down in the driver's seat.

"I didn't really know how else to put it," she said.

"Do you love him, Dusty?"

Her cheeks warmed, and she was thankful for the darkness of the night. This wasn't any of Chad's business, but for some reason, she wanted to talk. She wasn't quite ready to say the actual words. Not to Chad, anyway. "I-I don't know. I've never been in love before."

"Neither has Zach."

"Not even with Angelina?"

Chad scoffed. "*Especially* not with Angelina."

"But they were engaged."

"So?" He turned the key in the ignition. "Look, Zach and I, we're cowboys. We don't talk about this sort of thing. In fact, he'd probably whoop my ass if he knew I was telling you any of this. But I know my brother like the back of my hand. He's in love with you. I'd stake my fortune on it."

"Let's just get to the hospital, Chad."

"Agreed." He backed out of the parking lot. Then, "There's something else I'd stake my fortune on."

"What's that?"

"You're in love with him, too."

★ ★ ★

Dusty sat in the hospital waiting room, leaning into Chad's hard form. Laurie sat on Chad's other side, her worried eyes sunken and sad. None of them spoke.

"Sam!" Dusty jumped up and ran into her brother's arms as he entered. "Thanks for coming."

"What's going on? How's he doing?"

"No news yet," Chad said, "but it shouldn't be too much longer."

"Can I get any of you all anything?" Sam asked. "Coffee or something?"

Dusty shook her head.

"Nothing for me, bud," Chad said.

"How about you, Ms. McCray?"

"Nothing, sugar. And please, call me Laurie, Sam."

Sam sat down next to Dusty and took her hand. "He'll be all right, Dust."

She nodded and gulped down a sob.

After what seemed like hours, Zach's doctor finally entered. "Mrs. McCray," he said.

"Yes. How is he?" Laurie asked.

"So far, so good. His wound is infected, so we have him on IV antibiotics. It's probably just a local staph infection, fairly common with this type of injury, but because of his high fever, we want to err on the side of caution. I have him on three different medications, plus a sedative."

"I see."

"It's lucky you got him here when you did. His fever was nearly one hundred and five degrees. If it had gone any higher, he could have had a seizure."

Dusty nearly lost her footing. "Lord..."

"Thank God you were with him, sugar," Laurie said. Then, turning back to the doctor, "How quickly do you expect him to respond?"

"Within twenty-four hours if all goes as planned. We'll keep an eye on him. He's not in any immediate danger that I can see, so you all can go home and get some rest if you want."

"I'm not leaving," Dusty said. "I'll stay with him."

"He's not responsive, ma'am," the doctor said. "He's sedated."

"I don't care. I'm staying. I'll sit with him."

"It's the middle of the night, Dust," Sam said.

"Do I look like I care? I said I'm staying."

"I think he'd like her to be here, Sam," Chad said and turned to Laurie. "Come on, Ma. I'll take you back to the hotel.

We can get a few hours of sleep and then we'll come back."

"You should go too, Sam," Dusty said. "You're competing tomorrow."

"Yeah, I know."

"I'm sorry I won't be there."

"It's okay. I understand. You need to be here."

She nodded. "You'll be great. But you need some sleep. You can still get a few hours."

"I've busted broncs on less sleep than this. I'll be fine."

"Just the same—"

"Yeah, I'll go. If you need me, just call."

Left alone in the waiting room, Dusty walked down the corridor to Zach's private room. He lay on the bed, covered, one arm on top of the sheets hooked to an IV drip. Dusty moved the vinyl recliner in the corner next to the bed and sat down, taking Zach's hand in hers. "I'm here," she whispered. "I'm here, sweetheart."

She thought she felt him squeeze her hand.

★ ★ ★

He awoke for a few minutes after dawn. Dusty brought his hand to her lips and kissed his fingertips. "Hey there," she said.

"Hey."

"How're you feeling?"

"Been better," he rasped. "Water?"

"Right away." She quickly poured a cup from the pitcher on his night table and held it to his lips. "Here. Drink, sweetheart."

"What happened?" he asked.

"Your leg is infected. You had a really high fever last night."

"I'm sorry, darlin'."

"Stop being silly. There's nothing to be sorry about."

"I wanted to love you all night."

"You just concentrate on getting better. They're drugging you with all kinds of meds, and you'll be back on your feet in no time."

"I'm glad you're here."

"There's nowhere else I'd be."

His parched lips curved upward slightly.

Dusty kissed his forehead. He was sweaty and clammy, but still quite hot. "I'll be right back," she said. She went to the bathroom and wet a cloth with cool water. When she returned, she pressed it to his forehead.

"That's nice," he said.

"Just relax."

"My sweet darlin'." He sighed. "I love you."

A tear fell down Dusty's cheek. Was he aware of what he had just said? "Sleep, Zach." Dusty pressed her lips to his in a soft kiss. When she lifted her head, his eyes were closed.

His poor lips were cracked and dry, so Dusty grabbed a tube of lip balm out of her purse and smeared some on his lips. She remoistened the cloth and placed it on his forehead again.

A nurse came in a few minutes later to change his IV drip. "Is it time for more medication?" Dusty asked.

"Yes. Time for the next dose," she said.

"How's he doing?"

"So far, so good."

"His fever doesn't seem to be going down." Dusty smoothed Zach's hair. "He's still so hot."

"It hasn't been that long," the nurse said. "If he's not improving by this evening, you can worry. For now, you should get some rest."

Dusty sighed. Sleepiness tugged at her. When the nurse left, she crawled into the bed with Zach and snuggled up against him, her derriere hanging off the edge of the mattress. She breathed in his masculine aroma and tried to relax.

★ ★ ★

Evening arrived, and Zach was still burning with fever. Dusty sat in the waiting room with Laurie, Chad, and Sam. When the doctor approached, she stood up.

The doctor cleared his throat. "I'm afraid he hasn't responded to the antibiotic treatment as hoped."

Neither Dusty nor Laurie spoke.

"What's the next step then?" Chad asked.

"Put him on stronger antibiotics. And we'll culture the wound, see what grows. It's obviously something that's resistant to the antibiotics we've tried so far. The main thing is to watch for necrotizing fasciitis."

"What's that?" Laurie asked.

"It's commonly referred to as the flesh-eating bacteria. It's associated with streptococcus A, which is the bacteria that causes strep throat, but it can actually be caused by several different bacteria."

Dusty gulped. This didn't sound the least bit good. "I need to go to him," she said.

"He won't know you're there," the doctor said.

"I don't care."

"Dusty." Sam pulled her aside. "I need to talk to you for a minute."

"What? What is it, Sam?"

"I shouldn't have to tell you this, because you already

know it. But you can't stay with him, Dust. Not if he has some kind of highly contagious bacteria growing in that wound. Your white cell count is up. We don't know what's going on with it yet, but your immune system could be compromised. You could be highly susceptible to infection."

Dusty was well aware of that fact. "It doesn't matter. I'm going to stay with him. I'm the reason he's here in the first place. He needs me."

"He doesn't need you to get sick because of him."

"But he's sick because of me! This is all my fault, Sam. I couldn't live with myself if I left him."

"Come on, Sis, you know he wouldn't want you to put yourself in danger."

"Sam, I've already decided that I'm leaving once he's well. And he *will* get well, damn it. But until he's well, I need to stay."

"You've decided to leave him?"

"Yeah." She sniffed as a tear fell. "I won't saddle him with a sick woman who can't ever give him a family. He deserves more than that. So much more. But for now, he needs me. I... I don't think he'll get well unless I'm here."

"Jesus Christ. You're in love with him."

"No, that's not it." But it was a lie. She knew it, and judging from the look on Sam's face, he did, too. "Yes. Yes, I am." Saying it out loud made it so final. So true. "And it's because I love him that I'm going to leave him, but not until he's well."

"Even if it costs you your own health? You love him that much?"

"Yes." Without a doubt.

"I sure as hell hope he's worth it, Dust."

"He is. Now if you'll excuse me, I'm going to go to the man I love."

Without speaking further to the doctor or to Laurie and Chad, Dusty headed back to Zach's room. He looked so peaceful in his drug-induced sleep, but when she looked more closely, the underlying tension in the smooth lines of his face showed itself. She caressed his beard-roughened jaw, leaned forward, and kissed his lips.

"I'm here, sweetheart," she said. "I'm not leaving until you're well. I love you. I love you so much." Tears rolled down her cheeks. "I'm so sorry about all of this. I wish I'd never come to Denver. If I hadn't, you wouldn't be here in this stupid hospital, and I wouldn't have to break your heart and mine." She lay down next to him, cuddled into his body, and sobbed into his shoulder.

After ten minutes, she choked back her last sob, determined to focus on Zach and not herself. "I'll see you well if it's the last thing I do. I will, Zach. I will."

CHAPTER THIRTEEN

Twenty-four hours later and still no change. The culture hadn't shown anything other than strep and staff, but Zach wasn't responding to antibiotics. Worse still, the infection appeared to be spreading.

"I'm going to take him into surgery," the doctor told them. "I need to remove some of the diseased tissue."

"Will there be scarring?" Laurie asked.

"Some. The extent will depend on how much I have to take."

"But he's so weak from fever," Laurie said. "Can he handle surgery?"

"He's young, healthy, and in great physical shape. Trust me, I've operated on much worse and they've come through fine. I think it's the best alternative at this point."

Dusty sat, dazed, running her fingers through her greasy hair. It had been two days since she had bathed. She hadn't eaten properly, and she was walking around like a zombie. She said nothing to the doctor, just watched him walk away in a blur. She blinked. Her eyes wouldn't focus.

"Come on, twerp," Chad said. "I'll take you to your hotel. You need a bath and a good night's sleep."

"I'm not leaving him."

"How about if I take you to Zach's suite? Would you like that?"

"Only if he's there."

Chad sighed. "All right."

Dusty closed her eyes and prayed silently to a God she wasn't sure existed to please spare Zach's life. She was tired, so tired. Her body ached with fatigue, and a fog swam in her mind. Sam had taken third place bronc busting, but when he came to the hospital to tell her the news, she hadn't been able to so much as smile for him.

"Sugar." Laurie touched her arm.

Dusty opened her eyes.

"Come with me," Zach's mother said. "It's not good for us to sit around doing nothing like this."

She led Dusty to the women's room and produced two small bottles of shampoo and conditioner from her purse. "Lean down. I'm going to wash your hair."

The thought that it would make more sense to use the shower in Zach's room floated on a synapse across Dusty's mind, but she nodded at the older woman. She didn't have the strength to argue. Laurie's gentle touch on Dusty's scalp soothed her, and she nearly nodded off. When Laurie finished she wrapped Dusty's head in a towel and handed her a jar of Noxzema. "Wash your face now."

Dusty did as she was told. It did feel better to be clean.

"You have beautiful hair," Laurie said, as she combed through it. "You always did, even when you were a babe. Such a lovely strawberry-blond color. So thick and wavy."

Dusty said nothing.

"Your mama had beautiful hair, too. Hers was lighter than yours, but still lovely."

Dusty choked back a sob.

"I'm sorry, sugar. Does it bother you to talk about your mama?"

Dusty shook her head. Selfish and vain as she was, she wasn't crying for her mother, or even for Zach, at that moment. She was crying over her hair. Zach loved her hair, and she was going to lose it.

Again.

"Why are you being so nice to me?" she asked Laurie. "This is all my fault. If I hadn't been on Diablo, Zach wouldn't have gotten hurt. If I were you, I'd hate me."

Laurie touched Dusty's shoulders, the warmth penetrating through her wrinkled blouse. "I suppose it would be easier if I had someone to blame," she said. "The truth is, Zach didn't blame you. Oh, he was angry, no lie, but when it came down to it, his only concern was for you, even after he got hurt. My son cares for you. Frankly, I was beginning to wonder if he'd ever care for a woman the way his father cared for me. If you were able to reach him on that level, all I can do is love you. No matter what."

Dusty fell into Laurie's arms and sobbed.

"There now. He's going to be all right."

Laurie's motherly touch offered no solace. Dusty cried for own mother, for herself, and for Zach. Mostly for the love she would never have.

★ ★ ★

"I wish I could do something," Angelina said to Chelsea. They sat in the waiting room, awaiting news of the outcome of Zach's surgery. Dusty had disappeared with Laurie, Chad and Dallas had gone for coffee, and Angelina was thankful for the chance to speak freely.

"You're here. That's all that matters," Chelsea said.

"I should be the one staying in his room with him, not her."

"Honey, have you seen her? She looks like she's been run over by a truck. Do you really want that?"

"No, but..." Angelina sighed. "I just wish I could help him."

"You really care about him, don't you?" Chelsea's raised eyebrows indicated the other woman's surprise.

"Of course I do," Angelina said. "Why would I want to be with him otherwise?"

"Yes, of course," Chelsea said.

Angelina regarded her friend. Chelsea looked perfect as usual, dressed in tailored clothing accented with a Prada handbag and shoes. Angelina enjoyed clothes as much as the next person, but having grown up on a ranch, they weren't as important to her as they seemed to be to Chelsea. For Chelsea, appearance was paramount.

For the first time, Angelina wondered if Chelsea loved her husband. Why wouldn't she? Dallas was gorgeous. And loaded. Slightly taller than Zach, but not quite as tall as Chad. About six-three, and his black hair streaked with silver was rugged perfection. Yet she had never seen much affection pass between him and his wife.

Dallas was removed. That was the only way Angie could think to describe him. He didn't seem close to anyone. Not his brothers, his mother, or his wife. Part of him was shut off from everything else. What was it that kept him closeted from those he should be closest to?

"Chelsea, can I ask you a personal question?"

"Sure."

"Are you and Dallas in love?"

Chelsea rolled her eyes. "Of course we are. We're married, aren't we?"

Angelina nodded, but she wasn't convinced. Marriage didn't equal love. No. Love wasn't a requirement for marriage.

But it should be. It definitely should be.

"I've been thinking," she said.

"About what?"

"Maybe Zach and I aren't meant to be."

"Are you kidding me? What have we been working toward all this time?"

"I know." She sighed. "And I appreciate all your help. Really, I do. But..." She took a deep breath. "Zach's not in love with me."

"So? Get the license and worry about love later."

Angelina couldn't believe what she was about to say. "I'm not sure I want that." In her heart, she knew she spoke the truth.

Chelsea tapped her Prada-clad toes on the tile floor. "Suit yourself, then. I would have loved to have you for a sister-in-law."

"Yeah, it would have been fun." Though Angelina wasn't sure she meant the words anymore. Was Chelsea truly that shallow? And had she, Angelina, been on the same road? "I'm still going to stick around and help Zach through this. I want him to know I'm here for him. That I care."

Chelsea's gaze wandered. She had clearly grown bored with the conversation. "Of course," she said.

Angelina looked the other way, staring at the abstract art on the wall. All red with black splotches. Kind of the way she felt inside.

★ ★ ★

On the second night after his surgery, Dusty awoke in the chair next to Zach, her hand soaked with sweat from his. She scrambled to call the nurse, who came quickly.

"Please, you need to check his temperature. I think... I think his fever broke."

"Looks that way." The nurse smiled as she held the thermometer to Zach's ear. "Ninety-nine point two. A little high, but I'd say it's perfect."

"Thank God, thank God." Dusty buried her face in her hands.

"He's going to be hungry when he wakes up," the nurse said as she pulled down the sheet and removed Zach's catheter. "It's the middle of the night, but I think we should find some food for him. What does he like?"

"He likes meat and potatoes. Manly food." Manly food for her manly man.

"I'll see what I can do. In the meantime, I need to change his linens. These are soaked."

"I'll help you."

"Oh, there's no need."

"Please, I want to."

The nurse's gaze fell to Dusty's wringing hands. "Honey, the best thing for you right now would be to go home and get some sleep. You've been here nonstop."

"I'm not leaving. At least not until he wakes up and I know he's okay."

The nurse shook her head, smiling. "He's lucky to have you. You sure do love him, don't you?"

Dusty nodded. Warmth flowed through her. "More than

anything." She pulled the corner of the sheet out from the mattress. "How exactly do we...?"

"He's a big one, isn't he?" The nurse tidied Zach's end table. "Maybe it'd be better if we wait until he wakes up. He'll probably feel like getting up. That'll make it easier."

At that moment, Zach's eyelids fluttered. Dusty sat down on the edge of the bed and took his hand. "Hey."

"Hey." His voice was hoarse and raspy. "Thirsty."

The nurse poured a cup of water and held it to Zach's lips. He took a few shallow sips. The nurse excused herself to see to his food.

"You sure scared us, Zach," Dusty said, stroking his fingers with her own.

"Sweet darlin', I'd never leave you."

His words sliced into her heart like a knife. She was caught between the giddiness of knowing he was well and the heart-wrenching anguish of knowing she had to leave him soon. She'd break his heart. But she couldn't think about that now. She had to see him out of the hospital and safely back to his hotel suite. Then she'd go home to Montana.

"What do you feel like? Are you hungry?"

"Yeah. A little."

"I've got the nurse looking for meat and potatoes for you." She brought his hand to her lips and kissed it.

"Got any more of those?" he asked.

"Meat and potatoes?"

"Nah. Kisses."

She smiled. "I think I might have a few."

"Come here then." He urged her forward. "I hope you don't mind me lookin' like death warmed over."

She shook her head, a tear forming in her eye. "You've

never looked more wonderful to me."

She pressed her lips to his. They were dry and chapped, but they felt like heaven against her own. He wrapped his arm around her neck and pulled her closer. She sighed as his tongue eased her lips open. She responded, even knowing he shouldn't be exerting himself. After a few breathless moments, she pulled away.

"Don't strain yourself."

"I'm not."

She bit her lip, worried. "I don't want you to get too turned on."

"Too late." He pointed to the sheet at his waist, tented by his obvious erection.

"Zach—"

"Hey, I'm only human. Kissing my woman has that effect on me."

"Oh, Zach." Dusty's eyes misted. "I was so worried about you."

"Please don't cry. I can bear anything but your tears."

"But it was all my fault. If anything had happened..."

"I'm too ornery to die, darlin'."

"That's not funny, Zach."

"I'm sorry. Come here."

He opened his arms, and she lay down next to him, soggy sheets and all.

"You know I love you, don't you?"

She nodded, nuzzling into his neck, still clammy from sweat. She wanted to say it back, but it would just make things harder for both of them.

"Did you stay with me the whole time?"

She nodded again.

"I thought so. Somehow, I knew you were here."

"Are you in any pain, Zach? Can I get you anything?"

"All I want is you."

"Not even some meat and potatoes?"

"Well, maybe. I am feeling a little gaunt."

"You look absolutely beautiful."

"So do you."

She glanced down at her wrinkled clothes and shook her head. "I'm a mess. Thank God Sam brought me a toothbrush and enough underwear so I could change every day."

"Maybe they'll let me out of here come morning."

"Don't bet on it. You were very sick, Zach. You had a really high fever for several days. And surgery. I was so scared."

"I'm sorry."

She laid her fingers over his mouth. "Stop saying that. None of this is your fault. It's all mine."

"You stop saying that, too. And kiss me again."

She lifted her lips to his. After another long kiss, she said, "Do you feel like you can get out of bed? I'd like to change your linens. They're soaked from when your fever broke."

"I might be able to. I have to piss like a racehorse."

Dusty rose from the bed to help him. "That's probably just irritation from your catheter. The nurse just took it out."

Zach winced.

Dusty smiled and looked around. "I don't see any crutches in here. I'll get some from the nurse, but for now, don't put too much weight on your leg, sweetheart. You'll have to lean on me."

"I like it when you call me that. Sweetheart." His face was pale and his eyes sunken, but his smile still made her heart leap. Breathtaking.

"Me too. Come on, now. I'll help you to the bathroom."

While Zach took care of business, Dusty hurriedly stripped the bed and replaced the soiled linens with the clean ones the nurse had left. When she finished, she knocked on the bathroom door.

"You can come in, darlin'."

He was sitting on the toilet seat putting toothpaste on a toothbrush.

"Do you want me to help you wash your hair or anything?" she asked.

"I know I must look like hell, but I don't feel up to it right now. I just want to brush my teeth."

"Okay."

When he had finished, she helped him back into bed and lay down next to him. "Go to sleep now, sweetheart." She kissed his lips lightly. "I'll wake you when the food gets here."

She snuggled into his chest, and he was already breathing steadily in slumber.

"I love you," she whispered.

CHAPTER FOURTEEN

A little less than forty-eight hours later, Zach was back in his hotel suite, freshly showered and shaved. Chad was competing in a bull riding competition, and his mother had gone along to watch. Angelina hovered about, begging to help him. He finally sent her out to fill a prescription and hoped she'd take her time about it. He wanted Dusty, but she had left as soon as he got back to his room, and he hadn't seen her since. He had called her hotel, but she hadn't been in. If only she had a cell phone. He was pretty sure Sam would be at the rodeo for Chad's ride.

Dusty was still hiding something from him. She hadn't said she loved him yet, but he was pretty sure she did. At this point, he didn't much care if she ever said it. He wanted to be with her and that was that, but they needed to settle a few things. The stock show would be over in two days, and he planned to take Dusty home with him.

Angelina returned with his medication, and he sent her away again for some food. He reached for his cell from the night table and dialed the Holiday Inn again, asking for Dusty's room.

"I'm sorry, sir," the clerk said. "The O'Donovans checked out an hour ago."

"What?"

"They checked out."

"You must be mistaken. The stock show isn't over."

"They canceled their reservation for the rest of their stay.

I'm sorry, sir."

Zach hung up and threw his cell phone on the floor. There had to be some mistake. She wouldn't leave without telling him. Would she?

He scrambled out of bed, cursing at the pain in his thigh, and pulled on a pair of jeans and a T-shirt. He grabbed his crutches and limped down to the parking garage and drove his rented Jag over to the stock showgrounds. He had a hunch...

Yep, she was there. By Diablo's pen, singing to that damn bull again. Hell, she'd leave without saying goodbye to him, but he knew she wouldn't be able to resist seeing that goddamned animal one last time.

His eyes burned as he walked toward her. "You checked out of your hotel," he said, his voice sounding low and primal.

"Zach." Her brown eyes widened into two saucers. "Y-You shouldn't be out of bed."

"You were going to leave. You were going to fucking leave me, weren't you?"

"I..." She fidgeted with a stray wisp of hair that had come loose from her braid.

He dropped his crutches and stalked closer to her, the heat of his own anger overpowering the pain in his leg. "Answer me, goddamn it!"

"Please. Don't hurt yourself."

"Answer me!"

"I'm not worth this, Zach. The last thing I want—"

"The last thing *you* want?" He gripped her shoulders and she winced. He didn't care. "Have you given a thought to what *I* want? In case you haven't, let me spell it out for you. Y-O-U. You, Dusty. I want *you*. But you already know that. Why are you leaving me?"

"I-I never should have come here."

"Well, you did, and I'm not giving you up."

"You don't have a choice, Zach."

"The hell I don't." He dropped one hand to her wrist and dragged her toward his rented hay barn next to Diablo's stall, ignoring the piercing sparks in his leg.

"Stop this. You'll hurt yourself."

"Don't righteously give a damn at the moment."

"I do, Zach. I give a damn. About you. About your leg. Your health."

"Darlin', if you gave a damn about me you wouldn't be leaving me." He dragged her into the barn and pushed her against the wall. "What kind of a game have you been playing with me?"

Her cherry lips trembled. "No game. I swear it."

"Bullshit, darlin'. I love you. I want to be with you. I could have sworn you felt the same. But you were going to leave me. Now explain yourself."

"There's nothing to explain. I...don't want you."

He didn't believe her for a minute. "That's crap." He jerked her face upward, forcing his gaze upon hers.

"No—"

He clamped his lips onto hers and thrust his tongue into her mouth. He wasn't in the mood to be gentle. He took from her, the ache between his legs unbearable in its heat. It overrode the pain in his thigh, the rational part of his brain. At that moment, his body wanted her body, and nothing else mattered.

He pushed her into the rough wood of the barn wall. She sagged against him, sinking into his body, fitting him in all the right places. When she wrapped her arms around him, her fingers tunneling in his hair, stroking his face, he knew she had surrendered. He broke his mouth away and trailed feathery kisses across her cheek, to her ear.

"Tell me you don't want me, darlin'. Tell me, and I'll stop."

She panted against him. Her pulse hammered against his lips, racing in synchrony with his.

"Tell me, Dusty. Say you don't want this. You don't want me."

"I—I—" Her voice cracked, her body shuddered.

"You have to say it."

"I... I can't."

She grabbed his face in her hands and pulled him to her mouth again. The kisses were pressing, demanding, a tangle of teeth and tongues. He reached for her braid, pulled the band out, and fingered her hair into those luscious waves he loved.

He tore his mouth from hers. "Don't braid your hair anymore," he said roughly. "I like it down."

She nodded, and he heard her gulp for air before she slammed her lips against his again. He fumbled with her shirt as they kissed, finally swearing under his breath as he ripped it apart and sent buttons scattering. Sweet God, her bra had a front clasp. The first one she had worn like that. He snapped it open, released her delectable breasts, bent his head, and sucked a cherry nipple into his mouth. She clamped her hands around his head, holding him to her as he suckled. Her breathy, sexy noises increased the pressure inside him until he was so hard he thought he would burst.

He pulled his lips from her nipple and cupped her cheeks, staring into her big brown eyes alight with fire.

"What do you want, Dusty?" he rasped. "Tell me what you want."

"You. Now." Her nimble fingers made short work of his belt buckle and yanked his zipper down. He hissed as his arousal escaped through the opening in his boxers.

"Take off your pants," he ordered.

Her arms and hands shook visibly as she removed her boots, unbuckled her belt, and unzipped her jeans. She jerked them and her underwear down her legs in one swoop. As she stepped out of them, he thrust his hand between her legs. Oh yeah, she was ready.

He tore off his boxers and lifted her, immune to the pain in his thigh as her legs wrapped around him. He backed up and the splintery wood scratched his back as he used the wall for support to hold his weight and Dusty's on his right leg. She reached down for his cock, but he shoved her hand aside and plunged himself into her.

"Zach!" she cried out, wrapping her hands around him, grabbing his bare ass, trying to pull him closer to her. Her gorgeous breasts pushed into his chest as he pumped into her. Her breath came in hoarse sobs as she buried her face in his shoulder.

His heart thumped unsteadily in his chest. He was close, so close, but damn it, he wanted his woman to come.

"Touch yourself," he commanded.

She made a breathy sound. "What?"

"I want you to come. I can't do it for you. All my weight's on one leg and it won't hold me if I move my arms. Touch yourself."

Do it fast. She was so tight and she hugged him so completely, so thoroughly, he knew he'd blow in a matter of seconds.

As soon as she pressed on her swollen nub, her spasms

hugged him. He thrust so far inside her he nudged the edge of her womb, and he came with a savage intensity he had never known.

"Mine," he said, his voice husky with smoke, his cock still throbbing. "You're mine." He rested his cheek on the top of her head, the soft red-gold tresses like a satin pillow. "You're coming home with me."

She panted against his shoulder.

"I need to put you down, darlin'. My leg..."

She jerked away from him. "Oh, God. I'm so sorry."

"Why? I'm not."

"Your leg. What was I thinking?"

He reached in his pocket and pulled out his bandana. "Here," he said, handing it to her. "For...you know."

She cleaned up and pulled on her panties and jeans. She clasped her bra and started to button up her shirt, but several buttons were missing.

"Sorry about that," Zach said.

"It's okay."

He scrambled into his boxers and jeans, sat down on a bale of hay, and pulled her into his lap, wincing at the pain in his thigh as he brushed his lips lightly over hers. He had been rough with her. Now he wanted to be gentle. To hold her and love her.

"Your leg, Zach."

"It's all right."

"No." She squirmed, trying to escape. "I don't want to hurt you. It's the last thing I ever wanted."

"Then don't leave me, darlin'. Please don't leave me."

"I'm so sorry," she whispered, tears trickling down her cheeks. She bounded up, and before he could react, she had grabbed her boots and run out of the barn.

He couldn't run, so he couldn't follow her. The pain in his thigh lanced through him like a gash from a sword.

But it was nothing compared to the agony in his heart.

CHAPTER FIFTEEN

Dallas McCray had a gnawing pain in his stomach that wouldn't go away. For a few days after the family returned to McCray Landing, he tried dousing it with Pepto-Bismol and Zantac, to no avail. Then, as he watched his brother mope around the ranch, working himself harder than he should while recovering from a gore injury, Dallas figured out the problem.

Guilt.

He had been wrong about Dusty O'Donovan. She hadn't been after Zach's money. Had she been, she would be here now. Zach had made no secret of the fact he'd wanted to bring Dusty back to McCray Landing with him, but she and Sam had gone back to Montana.

Dallas tried to understand what Zach must be feeling. Love. He wasn't sure he'd ever felt it, at least not the way Zach did for Dusty. His marriage to Chelsea had grown stale. They never talked, and they never spent time laughing or playing. They hardly ever made love anymore. Had he ever felt for Chelsea what Zach appeared to feel for Dusty? Would he be devastated, as Zach was, if Chelsea left him?

He sighed. He didn't know the answer to that question.

He needed to figure out his own marriage, but that would take more time than he had at the moment. In the meantime, he'd do what he could for Zach. He had a lot to make up for. Grabbing his cell phone out of his pocket, he called Chad.

"What's up, Dallas?" Chad's voice was always so full of

life.

"Hey, Chad. I have a favor to ask."

"Sure. What can I do for you?"

"You know that PI you used a couple years ago when your van was stolen?"

"Larry? Yeah."

"I need his number."

"I don't have it on me. Can I call you later?"

"Yeah. Er, no." Dallas fidgeted with a few coins in his pocket. Was he about to overstep a boundary? "Maybe you could call him, if you don't mind. Since you and he go way back. Wasn't he in your class?"

"Yep."

"I want to hire him."

"Is Chelsea running on you?"

"No, no. Nothing like that." Dallas hadn't even considered that possibility. He wasn't sure he gave a damn. "I want to check out Dusty O'Donovan. There's got to be some reason why she ran away from Zach."

"I had thought the same thing. The girl's in love with him. I'd bank on it."

"Then let's see what we can find out, okay?"

"Sure. I'll call Larry as soon as I get back home. He ain't cheap, though."

"Who cares?"

"Not me." Chad laughed. "I'll get in touch with you tomorrow after I talk to him."

"Great."

"No problem."

Dallas breathed in and swallowed a gulp of air. "Hey... Chad?"

"Yeah?"

"Did you and Zach really hate me growing up?"

"Dallas, what the hell are you talking about?"

It was now or never for Dallas. He wanted to end his estrangement with his brothers. Chelsea had always been against him being close to his family. Yeah, that was reason enough to repair the bridge. He sighed into the phone. "You and he are so close, and I'm the odd man out all the time. I know I'm five years older than Zach and eight years older than you, but..."

"Brother, I'm gonna need a drink if we're trekking down memory lane."

"You want to meet me somewhere?"

"Whoa. You really want to talk, don't you?"

Dallas nodded, though he knew Chad couldn't see him. "Yeah. I think I do."

"You want me to call Zach?"

"Nah. He's got enough on his mind. I'll grab a bottle of Macallan out of the cabinet and meet you at your place. Will that work?"

"Sure enough. I'm on my way there now. You eaten?"

"Nope."

"I'll pick up a bucket of chicken. See you there in about half an hour."

"Sounds good." He hung up, deposited the phone in his pocket, and turned to see his wife. When had she come in?

"Who were you talking to, Dallas?"

"Chad. I'm meeting him over at his place for dinner and a drink."

"Oh. I didn't realize you had made plans."

"Just made them two minutes ago. Did you need me here

for anything?"

"Well"—she fidgeted—"I was sort of hoping we could have dinner together."

"We haven't had dinner together in months, Chelsea, except when we were in Denver."

"If we're going to start a family, Dallas," Chelsea said, her voice a petulant whine, "we should act like one."

Dallas raked his fingers through his black hair. "If we're going to start a family, Chelsea, we need to have sex more than once a month."

"Exactly what do you mean by that?"

"What the hell do you think I mean by that? Jesus Christ. How do you expect to get pregnant when you put me off all the time? I'm a man. I have needs."

Chelsea tapped her foot indignantly and tugged on her lower lip with her teeth. "Are you cheating on me?"

"Hell, no." Dallas's pulse raced at the accusation. "A cowboy wouldn't do that. But I'm gettin' damn tired of Rosie and her four friends."

"That's disgusting." Chelsea grimaced.

"That's a fact of life," Dallas said. "Ninety-five percent of all men do it, and the other five percent lie about it."

"Ha-ha."

"Nothing funny about it from where I'm standing."

Chelsea reddened. The color crept up her neck, into her cheeks. Her blue eyes flashed. She was a beauty, his wife, but her sparkly perfection paled in comparison to the fresh country prettiness of Dusty O'Donovan. For the first time, Dallas envied one of his brothers. He wanted Zach to be happy. Dusty had left for a reason, and Dallas meant to find out what it was.

"Don't wait up for me," he said, heading for the door.

"What do you need to see Chad for?"

"He's my brother, and I want to spend some time with him."

"I'm your wife!"

"And you haven't indicated any interest in spending time with me until now. Sorry, I've already made plans."

"Don't you dare walk out that door, Dallas McCray."

"Is that a threat?"

Chelsea eased back a little. "I just want to know why you're going."

Dallas cleared his throat. "If you must know, Chad and I are going to find out why Dusty O'Donovan left Zach."

"Dusty O'Donovan? You're kidding. Angelina will take care of Zach. Dusty was nothing more than a fling."

"Angelina has backed off. She and Zach are over. And Zach is thirty years old. If this had been a fling, he'd be over it. He's in love with her, and I want him to be happy."

"With that piece of trailer trash?" Chelsea stomped her toe.

Dallas shook his head, disgusted. "You're something else, Chelsea. I'm outta here. Like I said, don't wait up."

He closed the door on his wife's fuming expression.

★ ★ ★

Dusty's stomach churned with nausea. And dread.

She had been home for nearly four weeks, and today was the day to have her follow-up blood work done. For the last week, she'd been feeling fatigued, but today she was downright ill. And sad. It could only mean one thing. The first blood test hadn't been a fluke. Her white cell count was up because her leukemia had returned.

She finished cleaning out the stalls and pushed her hair out of her face. It would have made so much more sense to braid the long waves like she used to, but for some reason she felt she should wear it down for Zach's sake. Stupid, she knew. Especially since it would likely all fall out in the next month or two.

Sam's head popped in the stable. "Ready to go, Dust?"

"Yeah, just let me wash up first."

After a quick shower, she joined Sam in the old Ford pickup, and they headed to the hospital for her blood test. Her oncologist, Dr. Lloyd, took them into his office after he had examined Dusty.

"What do you think, Doc?" Sam asked.

"Your sister's temperature is slightly elevated, but that in itself isn't a major concern. However, the fact that she's been fatigued, and now nauseated, is cause for worry, I'm afraid. There was no abnormality in the white cells in the last sample, but there was an increased number. Obviously, if today's sample shows the same thing, even if the cells aren't leukemic, we need to be on guard."

"And if she does have leukemic cells?" Sam hedged.

"She'll go back on chemotherapy to induce remission."

Dusty said nothing, content to let Sam question the doctor. She knew what was going on. She'd been there before.

"And if they're not leukemic?"

"If the white cell count is elevated, but there are no leukemic cells, we'll monitor her closely over the next several months. The good news is we've caught it early, whatever it is."

"She was so close to her five year mark," Sam said, the

softness of his voice revealing to Dusty how worried he was.

Dusty, on the other hand, felt numb. Numb and nauseated, but not worried. That would come later tonight.

"Yes, I know. It happens sometimes. But we don't know anything just yet. I should have the results of today's test by Monday."

"How am I going to get through this weekend, Sam?"

"We'll get through it, Dust." Sam rose and shook the doctor's hand. "Thanks, Doc. We appreciate your help and your concern."

"I wish I had better news for you. Perhaps I will, come Monday. I'll call you at home, Dusty, as soon as I know anything."

"Thank you, Dr. Lloyd."

"Come on, Dust." Sam linked her arm through his and they walked through the hospital parking lot to the pickup. "I'm taking you to lunch."

"We can't afford to eat out, Sam."

"We can just this once."

Dusty sighed. "I'm not hungry. Not in the slightest. In fact, I feel like I'd throw up anything you put in my stomach. So let's not waste the money, okay? I'll make you a sandwich at home."

Sam squeezed her hand. "All right. If that's what you want."

"It's what I want."

★ ★ ★

"I told you I'm busy," Zach said, resisting Chad's pull on his arm.

Chad ignored him and ushered Zach into his mother's

sitting room in her sprawling ranch house. "We need to talk to you."

"Not now. I'm expecting an important call from one of our distributors. I'm swamped."

"Too busy for your mother?" Laurie took his hand and led him to her settee.

"Can't sit," Zach said. "What is it you all want? I have work to do."

"All you've done is work since we got back from Denver," Laurie said. "You're lucky you didn't re-infect your wound. Now sit."

Zach huffed and sat down roughly in an armchair. "Fine. What is it?" He rubbed his chin, still not used to his short goatee.

"Chad and Dallas have some things to say to you."

"What is it? Let's get this over with so I can get back to what I was doing."

"Well," Chad said, "since you've been moping around here like a bull who just got his nuts cut off, Dallas and I decided to do something about it."

"I ain't been moping around. I've been carrying my weight."

"That's not what he means, and you know it," Laurie said. "Now hear him out."

"I made a phone call a couple weeks ago, to an old friend of mine from high school. Larry Parks. You remember him?"

"Hell, no."

"Sure you do. Geeky kid. Kind of short and freckled?"

"Whatever."

"Anyway, Larry's a big time PI in Denver now. Not cheap either. Course he gave me a break."

Zach rolled his eyes. "What the hell are you talking about, Chad?"

"He can uncover just about anything. But he has to leave his scruples at home sometimes..."

"This is becoming tedious."

"Big word, Harvard man." Chad chuckled. "Can't you just say boring?"

"Christ," Zach muttered.

"All right, all right." Chad fingered a few manila folders on Laurie's coffee table. "Larry owed me a favor, so I called him up and asked him to do a little investigating."

"And I should care about this because..."

"Because I had him investigate a little filly named Dusty O'Donovan."

"Goddamn it, Chad." Zach rose. He was pretty sure steam would shoot out his ears soon. "I ought to tan your hide."

"Aw, sit down. I'm bigger than you anyway."

"But not tougher."

"You can whoop my ass later. Besides, it was Dallas's idea."

Zach turned his scathing gaze on his older brother. "I'll whoop his ass too, then."

"Simmer down," Dallas said. "Before this goes any further, I have something to say."

Zach crossed his arms. "I stopped caring what you had to say twenty years ago."

"I know." Dallas cleared his throat. "I don't blame you, but after thirty years of being my little brother, I think you have the right to hear this once. I was wrong."

"About what?" Zach asked.

"Yeah, there have been so many things," Chad joked.

Dallas ignored Chad. "About Dusty, Zach. She wasn't

after your money."

"I think that's obvious," Zach said, "or she'd be here."

"She'd be here if she could, I think, and not because of your money. But I'll let Chad tell it. He's the one who got all the info from Larry. I think you'll find the story very interesting."

"Ma, you were in on this?" Zach asked Laurie.

"No, Zach, I wasn't. Chad and Dallas didn't tell me until they had gotten the report," Laurie said. "I think you need to listen to what they have to say. It'll explain a few things."

"Look, I already know that her ranch needs money. I offered to help her. She turned me down. She left me. She doesn't love me. It's over. Kaput. Finito. The end."

"Just give me a few minutes to explain what Larry found out," Chad said. "Then, if you're not interested in learning more, we'll call it over."

"Please, Zach," Laurie said. "For me."

Zach relented and sat back down in the chair. "Go ahead."

"Turns out Mollie O'Donovan's parents were killed in a car wreck about ten years ago," Chad said. "They left the ranch to Sam and Dusty. Sam was a senior in high school, and Dusty was only thirteen, so Sean-Patrick, their dad, took care of the ranch for them. It's a small parcel outside of Black Eagle, about a hundred acres or so. It was never a big operation, but Sean did okay. Raised some beef, trained some cutters. Trained Dusty as a barrel racer and Sam on bronc busting. You know that."

"Yeah."

"Anyway, Sam went off to school at the university, majored in agriculture, came back, and Dusty started college. She had a scholarship. Smart as a whip, that one. It's well-known around the area that she's some kind of mathematical genius, as well as a wizard with animals. She could even rival your brains, I reckon."

"Keep talking."

"Anyway, she dropped out of school after a year."

"Because of money?"

"Hell, no. She had a scholarship, remember?"

"Then why'd she quit?"

"She got sick."

"So?"

"I mean *really* sick. Acute lymphocytic leukemia."

Zach jerked forward. "What?"

"A.L.L. Same thing Mollie died from."

"Oh my God..."

"Unlike Mollie, though, Dusty evidently responded to conventional treatment. She did chemo and went into remission. This was about five years ago."

"That can't be right. It's got to be a mistake. How did you find all this out?"

"The A.L.L. and the chemo are common knowledge, but as I told you, Larry sometimes leaves his scruples at home."

"Meaning?"

"Meaning"—Chad picked up one of the manila folders from the coffee table—"I have Dusty's medical records."

Zach rose again, his temper storming through his body. "How the hell?"

"I don't ask. I just take the information and pay Larry's bill."

Zach grabbed the folder from Chad and threw it to the floor. "That's a huge violation of Dusty's privacy. Not to mention illegal, Chad."

"So you don't want to know the details then?"

"No, I don't."

"Zach," Laurie said, "I don't condone this invasion of Dusty's privacy, but I think you should listen. It'll help you understand why she left you."

He sat. He couldn't help the curiosity that flowed through him. His Dusty, sick? He had to know what happened. "Fine. Go ahead."

"You're sure?" Chad asked.

"For Christ's sake, Chad, speak!"

"It turns out A.L.L. has a pretty good survival rate. For some reason, Mollie didn't respond, but Dusty did. She only needed four months of chemo and she was in remission."

"God." The thought of Dusty having to endure even one second of chemo broke his heart.

"A.L.L. is actually more common in kids than adults," Chad continued. "So it's pretty weird that both Mollie and Dusty got it as adults. Could be genetic, but nothing in the records indicates that there's any basis for that. Anyway, the chemo doesn't have a lot of lasting effects in kids, but in adults, there are things that occur pretty frequently."

"Such as?"

"Infertility, Zach. Dusty can't have children."

"Fuck." Zach buried his head in his hands. As much as Dusty loved animals, he had a hunch she loved kids even more. "They know for sure she's infertile?"

"It's pretty likely. The records are full of references of irregular periods. She's only had like four periods since she was sick. They're pretty sure she's infertile."

"Damn, it must have killed her to find that out."

"I imagine," Laurie said. "That girl's a born mother if I ever saw one. The way she fusses over animals. It was apparent even when she was a small child."

"None of that matters to me," Zach said. "I never told her I wanted kids."

"But you do," Laurie said.

"Well, yeah, I do. But we could adopt. I'd rather have Dusty."

"The story's not over yet, bro."

"There's more?" Zach clenched his jaw. He wasn't sure he could take anymore.

"Unfortunately, yes."

"Go on."

"Well, you've gotta know that chemo ain't cheap. The O'Donovans didn't have any health insurance."

"Oh, fuck."

"Yeah. Sean was determined that Dusty would get the best care available, especially after what happened to Mollie. He needed money, and he needed it quickly, because as you can imagine, you don't mess around with cancer. You treat it as soon as you find it. Anyway, he got involved in some shady business dealings that went awry. He damn near lost everything. The ranch ended up mortgaged to the hilt. They had to sell everything—the cattle, the animals, even some of the property itself. The only thing of value they kept was Dusty's barrel racer, Regina. I guess old Sean couldn't bear to take the mare away from his sick daughter. You know how Dusty loves animals."

"It must have killed her to sell Regina to Harper Bay," Dallas said.

"She sold her horse to Harper Bay?" Laurie shook her head.

"Yeah," Zach said. "Go on, Chad."

"Anyway, Sean kind of wilted away after that. He died

within a year of Dusty's remission. Word around Black Eagle is he died of a broken heart, if you believe that sort of thing. But there are some who say he took his own life."

"What?"

"Larry couldn't find any solid proof. Probably only Sam and Dusty know what really happened to their pa."

"I suppose so."

"Anyway, around the time Dusty was doing her chemo, a neighbor of hers bought a stud bull. Dusty was over visiting and took to the animal. That's how the whole Bull Whisperer thing started. It seems working with the bulls kept Dusty focused, so she didn't succumb to the fatigue and depression that's so common in cancer patients. Turns out she has a unique gift with bulls, as we all know now from experience."

"I'm thankful she found something that was cathartic for her," Laurie said.

"Yeah, it no doubt helped when her pa died too," Dallas said.

Zach swallowed and took a deep breath. "I knew she needed money. I would have gladly given her everything I have. I never told her I wanted a boatload of kids. I don't care that she's a cancer survivor. She's well now, so why did she leave me? It still doesn't make any sense. Unless she just didn't feel the same way about me that I feel about her."

"I'd wager that she does, bro," Chad said.

"How so?"

"There's a little more to my story."

The ominous look in Chad's brown gaze told Zach the news wouldn't be good. He buried his face in his hands. "What is it?" he mumbled.

"Turns out Dusty was nearing her five year mark as a

cancer survivor. If you hit five years out from A.L.L., you're considered cured. She had a blood test shortly before she and Sam came to Denver for the stock show."

"And?"

"It showed an elevated white count. Her records show a message was left for her at the Holiday Inn in Denver, and she called and got the information the day before her barrel race."

The day he found her by Diablo's pen, Zach thought. *The day we made love for the first time.*

Everything was falling into place now. Her statement that there were things worthy of her fear, but Diablo wasn't one of them. She'd said short hair wasn't flattering on her. She meant no hair. She'd said she couldn't get pregnant, that he deserved better. It all made sense. But why hadn't she told him? He had opened up to her, professed his love to her.

"God, she can't be sick again. She can't be." Zach buried his face in his hands. Profound sadness threatened to consume him.

"If she is, Zach, she needs you more than ever," his mother said.

"Dusty was supposed to go in for a recheck in three weeks, which is just about now," Chad said.

"You don't have those records?"

"'Fraid not."

"And no health insurance." Zach sighed, remembering how he had paid her bill for her concussion.

"Nope."

"No wonder she sold her mare to Harper. And she wanted that purse for riding Diablo. It wasn't the ranch. It was her life." Zach stood and began to pace.

"There's something else you should understand," Chad

said.

"What?"

"Her white count was up when you were in the hospital with your infection. She had to know what a huge risk she was taking by staying with you. You were growing God-knows-what kind of gunk in your leg, and she had a depressed immune system. She risked her health to be with you. To take care of you."

"She never left your side, Zach," Laurie said. "Not once."

"Why wouldn't she trust me with this? I told her I loved her, for God's sake!"

"I think she wanted to protect you, Zach," Laurie said. "You would have done the same for her."

"Protect me from what?"

"From having to deal with her illness. From the sadness of possibly losing her."

"Damn it all to hell," he said. "What good is all my land, my money, my stupid fucking Harvard education, if I can't save her?"

"Zach, sugar—" Laurie reached out to him.

"No, Ma. Stop right there."

He'd burn in hell before he let Dusty go through this alone. He'd be there for her, take care of her, love her. Whether she wanted him or not. Zach rose and strode toward the door.

"Now where are you going?" Dallas asked.

He faced them with a determined gaze. "I have to see Harper Bay about a horse, and then I'm going to go get my woman."

CHAPTER SIXTEEN

Sunday afternoon at the Double D Ranch found Dusty tending to one of the barn cats delivering a litter of kittens. A large litter—nine so far, and at least one more was on the way. The cat, a tabby Dusty called Jemma, was having trouble with this particularly large kitten. Dusty had called for the local vet in Black Eagle, but she was out of town. Sam was in Billings and wouldn't be back until late in the evening, so Dusty was on her own. She was concerned about the cat but secretly pleased that this blessed event required her staunch attention. It kept her mind off the news that was to come the next day.

"Come on, Jem, you can do it." Dusty massaged the cat's abdomen, trying to ease the delivery. Jemma squalled, but Dusty remained focused and tried to calm the cat and the newborn kittens searching for a teat.

When the last kitten still refused to budge, Dusty reached in to extract him manually. Jemma screeched but lay motionless, her belly pumping rapidly with breaths. Dusty turned the kitten carefully and at last withdrew him from his mother. Large, as she had expected, and black with caramel stripes. "We'll have to call you Fatso."

She checked Jemma and determined that Fatso was indeed the last kitten. Thank goodness. Poor Jemma was exhausted. She lay on her side, and once all the babies were nursing, Dusty stood up and wiped her hands on her overalls. What a mess.

But what a miracle. She loved newborns of all kinds. She sighed, knowing one of her own wasn't in the cards. Never would be.

Her hair, which she still wore down, hung in strings around her dirty face. Her clothes were filthy with afterbirth and mud. Yuck. She needed a shower, and she needed it now.

As she headed out the door of the barn and up the path to the small ranch house, she spied a blue pickup rolling into the drive. A pickup she had seen before. Had almost made love in.

Zach. Zach was here.

And she was covered in cat placenta.

She could run for the house, but he'd see her. She could run back to the barn, but when he found the house empty, that's the next place he'd look. Or she could just run.

But she didn't want to. Not this time. She was so tired of running from him. So tired of running, period. He had come for her, and she wanted him.

He stepped out of the truck, and her heart warmed when she saw he wasn't limping. She'd known he'd heal quickly. He was so vibrant and strong, so full of life.

He deserved a woman who could be his equal in that respect. Unfortunately, that wasn't her.

But he had come for her. Somewhere, in the back of her mind, she had known he would eventually. She had wanted him to. As he approached the door to her tiny home, she walked toward him. Then she couldn't help herself. She ran.

"Zach!" she cried out.

He turned, and his lazy smile lit up his gorgeous face. Oh God, he had grown a short goatee just like she'd asked him to. He looked incredible. So very incredible. All she could think about was how those short whiskers would feel against her cheeks when he kissed her.

And he *would* kiss her. It was written all over his face.

Within five seconds she was in his arms, his mouth on hers, their lips meshing together in frantic desperation. Her face was grimy and her hair not fit for human eyes, but he kissed her as though she were the last woman on earth. She kissed him back the same way.

After several timeless moments, Zach broke the kiss and pushed her away slightly, holding her shoulders. "You look beautiful," he murmured.

She couldn't help laughing at that observation. If she had ever doubted his love for her—and she hadn't—she'd have been convinced of it at that moment. "I just delivered a litter of ten kittens. I'm covered in blood and guts. Only you would say I look beautiful right now."

"You've never been anything but beautiful to me, darlin'." He ran his fingers through the thick tangles of her hair. "You're wearing your hair down."

She nodded.

"It'd be more convenient to wear it braided. You know, for doing ranch work." He grinned.

"Yeah, I know." Then, "You grew a goatee."

"Someone once told me I might look good with one." He winked.

"Someone was right," Dusty said.

"Why'd you leave me, darlin'?" He trailed his fingers down her cheek, down the curve of her neck. She shivered.

"It's a long story."

"Will you tell me? Will you let me help you?"

Dusty sighed. He had come all this way for her, and the reasons for keeping secrets no longer seemed important. She wasn't sure she could even remember them.

Oh, yeah. She didn't want to saddle him with a sick, infertile woman.

But maybe that was his decision to make, not hers.

"I'll tell you." She nodded. "I should have told you sooner. So come on in. The house is a sty. I haven't been feeling real well so I haven't done a lot of housework. I'm sorry..."

"I don't give a damn how clean your house is, Dusty. Is Sam at home?"

"He's in Billings. Said he'd be home around ten."

"Let's go in. I could use a cold drink."

"Of course. I should have offered you one. Where are my manners?"

"I don't give a damn about manners either, darlin', I'm just thirsty."

She led him into the house and pointed to the kitchen. "There's some soda and iced tea in the fridge. A couple of beers too, I think. I really need to take a quick shower and burn these overalls. Could you excuse me for a few minutes?"

"Sure. Take your time. I'll grab my duffel and get settled."

"You want to stay here?"

"Where else would I stay? Black Eagle's hardly a thriving metropolis. What is it, population nine hundred?"

"Nine seventy-eight, I'll have you know." She smiled and headed to her room to clean up.

Dusty's heart pounded as she stepped into the hot stream of water. The shower soothed her soiled skin, her tired muscles. She squeezed some shampoo into her palm, lathered it up, and spread it over her wet head.

"Allow me."

Zach was behind her, naked and glorious in his maleness.

He was even more beautiful than she remembered.

"What exactly are you doing?"

"Getting settled," he said.

"In my shower?"

"Can you think of a better place?"

"At the moment, no."

"As you will recall, I have a special talent for hair washing." He massaged her scalp. Between his strong hands rubbing her, his hard chest pressed against her, the steamy hot water, and the aroma of her herbal shampoo mixed with the aroma of Zach, she was in heaven.

She closed her eyes and breathed in deeply. "I've missed you so much, Zach."

"Then why did you leave me?"

She opened her eyes and stared into his. Their unique beauty was laced with sadness.

"I'll tell you. When we're out of the shower, okay? Right now, can we just relax?"

"Here, let me rinse you." He turned her and ran his fingers through her long tresses as the shower pelted the lather down the drain. She turned away from him, leaned her head back, and let the water stream push her hair from her face so it hung behind her in sopping locks. This time when she looked into his eyes, they smoldered. He pulled her to him and kissed her.

Their wet bodies slid together under the stream of the shower, and Dusty clamped her arms around Zach's neck as he hoisted her upward. She wrapped her legs around him and he entered her. So gently, so slowly. Not like in the hay barn at the stock show. This was lingering, soothing love. He pressed into her deeply, and she felt his sweet caress everywhere—in her heart, her soul, her very core. She clamped her mouth onto his and kissed him with passion, with all the love she felt for him. She did love him. So much.

Please, she begged silently. *Please don't let him be too disappointed.*

When he broke away, she whimpered, but he licked her earlobe and whispered endearments to her. Then he pushed her against the cool tiled wall of the bath and shoved into her more forcefully. "I love you, darlin'." He thrust, holding her rump in one hand while the other reached into her private curls. "I love you so much." He thrust again as he circled her clit with his thumb. "Please tell me you love me, Dusty. Please."

"Yes," she said in a breathless rasp. "Yes, I love you, Zach. I love you."

"Again," he groaned. "Say it again."

"I love you. I love you so much. Only you."

"I want to be your only lover, Dusty. The only man to come inside you. Please. Let me be the one."

Emotion swirled around her, in her. "Yes, I want that too. I want you to be the only one."

He plunged into her more deeply, taking, giving. "I want to take care of you."

He didn't know what he was saying, of course. But Dusty was determined to let him make the choice. "I love you," she said again, and then she climaxed. As her walls hugged him in the ultimate caress, she felt him come. She felt every spurt of his seed as he thrust.

And he told her loved her again.

★ ★ ★

"Put this on," Zach said, after they had dried each other

and he had pulled on a pair of boxers from his duffel. In his hand was a T-shirt.

"Uh, okay. What is it?"

"Just one of my shirts. The thought of my woman hanging out in one of my shirts has always kind of turned me on."

"I don't think you need any help in that department." Dusty raised her eyebrows at him. "But I love the idea of wearing your shirt." She pulled it over her head. "It's so big on me."

"Here." He handed her a pair of his boxers, and she stepped into them. He sat down on her bed and pulled her onto his lap. "Time to talk," he said.

"Yeah, I suppose so." Dusty fingered the red scar where Zach had been gored. There was an indentation where the surgeon had removed the diseased tissue, an interruption in his hair pattern. She stroked the flesh, smoothed her fingers along the ridges of scar tissue and then over the concave surface. "Does it hurt?"

"Not anymore, and the redness will fade with time."

"But you'll always have the scar."

"Yeah. I'll always have the scar."

"I'm so sorry."

"We've been through all that, darlin'. There's nothing to be sorry for." He pressed his soft lips to her neck. "Now. You love me."

"Yes. Yes, I do."

"I always knew it, anyway."

"Oh you did, did you?" She smiled and touched his cheek. "Confident of yourself, aren't you?"

"Just in love. It's a two-way street, you know."

"Yeah." She stroked his moustache. "I suppose it is."

"So why did you leave me?"

She sighed, holding her breath for a moment, gathering her courage. "I never wanted to leave you. Please believe that."

"Okay. I believe you. So tell me why you did."

"There were...that is, there *are* circumstances."

"They don't make any difference to me."

"You don't even know what they are yet." She punched him playfully.

"So?"

"Oh, Zach. If only things were different."

"Time to talk, darlin'. Tell me what's going on."

"It's such a long story, and you already know that our ranch is in financial trouble."

"Don't care. I have money. Keep talking."

"I love you, and I don't care about your money. I want you to know that."

"I do know that."

"Okay. The thing is, your money can't buy what I need, sweetheart."

"Which is?"

"My health. I'm sick, Zach."

"You look great to me." He smiled and brushed a damp tendril of hair out of her eyes.

"You're so sweet. The thing is, I...had cancer."

"I know."

"What? How did you know?"

"It's pretty common knowledge around Black Eagle, Dusty. You had leukemia. The same kind your ma died from."

"How long have you known?"

"Not long."

She tensed and moved ever so slightly backward. "And

you came for me anyway?"

He pulled her back, and her breasts brushed his chest. "What kind of a man do you take me for? Did you think I'd stop loving you because you had cancer? I'm a little pissed you'd think such a thing."

"No, I never thought that. It was more me. I'm the problem." Dusty's heart fluttered. Now was the moment of truth. She had to tell him, and she had to face the fact that he might not be able to handle it. "You see, there's a good chance the leukemia has returned."

Tears formed in her eyes, but he brushed them away. His touch was loving, concerned.

"Do you know for sure?"

"No. I get the results of my blood test tomorrow. But I had a test three weeks ago that showed an elevated white cell count, and I've been feeling like crap lately. I'm tired, and I've been sick to my stomach. Although I feel okay right now."

"Anything else?"

"I have a bruise on my thigh." She shifted so he could see the contusion.

"Just one bruise?"

"Yes. But I can't remember how I got it."

He chuckled. "You work your pretty bottom off on a ranch all day and you can't recall bumping your thigh?"

"This isn't funny."

"I know it's not." He fingered her hair, twirling it. "But Dusty, one bruise isn't anything to worry about."

"I suppose not, but along with the fatigue and the nausea, and my elevated white count a few weeks ago..."

"When do you find out tomorrow?"

"The doctor said he'd call as soon as he knew anything."

"Then we won't worry about it for now. Whatever tomorrow brings, we'll face it together."

"You still want me?"

"Christ, Dusty. What do you think?" He kissed her hard.

She broke away. "You don't know everything."

"What else is there to know?"

"I can't give you what you need, Zach. Even if I go into remission again."

"What is it that you think I need, other than you, darlin'?"

"A family. Babies, Zach. I can't give you a child."

"Because of the chemo?"

"Yeah. I'm infertile. It happens sometimes in women. It happened to me."

"I'm so sorry, darlin'. You'd have been a wonderful, loving mother. You still can be. We can adopt. Hell, we'll adopt a whole ton of kids if that's what you want."

"It's not the same."

"No, it's not." His tone was serious. "I'm sorry I won't be able to share that with you, to make a baby with you. Mostly because I know how much it would mean to you. But I still want you. I still love you."

Dusty clamped her arms around him and sank into his hard, warm chest. A giant anvil that had been hovering over her had suddenly disappeared. She kissed his neck, his ears, his beautiful face. "You're the most wonderful man in the entire world."

"Then I assume you'll want to marry me?" He smiled.

"If it's what you want, Zach."

"Don't you know me yet, woman? I don't say anything I don't mean. Tomorrow. We'll get married tomorrow. After we get the results of your test, we'll hightail it into Black Eagle, find the Justice of the Peace, and we'll get married."

"You want to marry me tomorrow?"

"Did you not hear me, woman? I never say anything I don't mean. Yes, I want to marry you tomorrow."

"But I might need more treatment. I might...not make it this time."

"Yes, you will."

"I'll lose my hair. You love my hair, Zach."

"Not more than I love you. Christ, Dusty."

"I'm sorry...but I just can't bear the thought of leaving you alone. I want more than that for you."

"Damn it, woman, there are no guarantees in life. I could be hit by a semi tomorrow. And if I am, I sure as hell want to be spending today with you!"

She burst into tears.

"Come on now, that's not fair." He brushed her cheeks with his thumbs.

"I love you so much."

"Then you'll marry me tomorrow?"

She sniffed, rubbing her nose on his shoulder. "Yes. I'll marry you tomorrow. I'd be honored to marry you tomorrow."

"Good. Now, how are you feeling? This very minute."

"Pretty well, actually. I was nauseated this morning, but since Jemma—she's the cat—went into labor, I've been feeling a lot better."

"Then put on your best outfit. I'm taking my woman to dinner."

"It's Sunday, Zach. Nothing in Black Eagle is open on Sunday. Small town, you know?"

"To hell with Black Eagle. We're driving into Billings. I already made the reservation at *Chez Nous.*"

"*Chez Nous?* That's so expensive."

"Darlin', there's something you need to understand about me."

"What's that?"

He winked at her. "I'm loaded."

She burst out laughing.

"Now that's a sweet sound."

"I love you."

"I love you, too. And there's something else you should know."

"What?"

"As soon as we're married, you'll be covered under my health plan, so you don't have to worry about your medical bills."

"But the leukemia is a pre-existing condition."

"Doesn't matter. I have a really good policy."

She hugged him tightly. "If you only knew how much I've been worried about all the bills, as well as everything else. You're my knight in shining armor, do you know that?"

"I'll settle for being the man you love, darlin'." He lifted her off his lap and patted her bottom. "Now get dressed. We'll worry about this other stuff tomorrow."

CHAPTER SEVENTEEN

Sitting at a candlelit table at *Chez Nous,* staring at her handsome and wonderful fiancé, who looked scrumptious in a blue-and-white striped button-down and navy Dockers, Dusty almost forgot about her blood test.

"Darlin'?"

"Hmm?"

"Could I talk you into telling me one more thing?"

"Maybe. What is it?"

"What exactly happened to your pa?"

Big jolt of reality. Dusty didn't like talking about her father, largely because she felt responsible for his situation. Rationally, she knew none of it was her fault, but her illness had been the catalyst.

She took a deep breath. "I once promised never to lie to you."

"You did."

"The truth is, my father killed himself."

Zach nodded solemnly, but said nothing.

"He swallowed a whole bottle of my pain pills, and he left a note for Sam and me." She stopped for a few seconds and then went on. "We've never told anyone about it, but I think most people probably know."

"Didn't the coroner figure it out?"

"He's an old family friend, so he didn't do an autopsy and he kept it quiet."

"I see."

"Papa got involved in some bad investments after I got sick. We didn't have any health insurance, and as you can guess, cancer treatment is expensive. He went a little crazy when I was diagnosed, probably because of what had happened to Mama. He was determined I was going to live, because he couldn't go through losing someone again."

"He loved you very much."

"Yeah. Yeah, he did. So he researched all the options for treatment. He actually considered sending me to the Mayo Clinic, until my oncologist in Billings assured him that my type of leukemia was fairly common as far as cancers go, and the treatment was standard and would be the same no matter where we went. Anyway, a couple months after I went into remission, Papa started selling off our livestock. I was still so happy to be well that I didn't ask a lot of questions. Soon we had nothing left. He let me keep Regina, though." She choked up, but took a drink of water and continued.

"After Papa died, Sam and I found out there were several mortgages on the ranch. He had left us a note saying he was sorry, that he knew we were young and strong and we'd be better off without him. Truth is, we needed him."

"I know." Zach nodded.

"We didn't have a lot of income coming in because the animals were gone. So we started competing in local rodeos and then we went regional. The stock show was our first national."

"Why'd you wait so long to go national? You're both real good."

"Money. You and your family probably don't think anything of the entry fees, but to us they were astronomical."

"You're right. I'm sorry."

"Anyway, I got paid a little for my work with local bulls as well, and that helped. Sam wanted to go out and get full-time work in Billings, but I couldn't handle the ranch myself, and we had worked so hard to keep it during the last four years since Papa died." She sighed. "That's about it in a nutshell."

"Well, your worries are over, darlin'."

"If only that were true."

"Yeah, if only. But at least your worries about money are over."

"How so?"

"What do you mean, how so? You'll come to Colorado and live on my ranch. I mean, *our* ranch."

"Of course I'll come with you. But I'm still half-owner of a bankrupt ranch, and I can't leave Sam to fend for himself."

"We'll figure something out." Zach played with Dusty's hand, entwining their fingers together across the table. "You all can sell the ranch, and Sam can come work for me."

"Maybe. But I think he'd rather have his own operation."

"Then he can work for me until he saves up enough."

A spark of hope bloomed in Dusty. "He might go for that."

"Or I'll loan him the money for his own ranch."

"Would you really?"

"Hell I'd buy it for him, to tell you the truth, but I know he wouldn't let me."

Dusty smiled. "No, he wouldn't, but it's sweet of you to be willing."

"Anything for you."

"I think I'm going to be a big expense for you, Zach."

"First of all, no, you're not. My insurance will pay your medical bills. Second of all, even if you were, I can't think of anything better to spend my money on."

Dusty smiled as two tears fell.

"Come on now, darlin', don't start the waterworks again."

"You're so good to me, and I feel so awful for…"

"For what?"

"For leaving you. I…I was so scared to stay. I loved you so much, so much that I wanted better for you than a sick woman, an infertile woman."

"Stop that right now."

"Please, let me finish. I felt terrible, like the world's biggest coward for trying to sneak away without telling you goodbye, but I was afraid if I went to you I wouldn't be able to leave, and I was convinced leaving was the best thing I could do for you."

"You were wrong."

"I *was* wrong. I made a decision that wasn't mine to make. It was yours. I should have told you the truth and let you decide. I'm sorry."

"It's okay, darlin'."

She smiled. "But I couldn't just up and leave. So I went to see Diablo. I thought if I said goodbye to him, I would be saying goodbye to you."

"Please don't say I look anything like that ugly cuss."

"He's a beautiful animal, but no, you don't look anything like him. It was just me being silly."

"The only silly thing you did was leave me. My heart broke right in two."

"I'm so sorry. Can you ever forgive me?"

"Maybe." His unusual eyes gleamed. "If you make love to me all night."

Dusty sipped her espresso. "I might be able to manage that. I'm feeling better tonight than I have in weeks. Thank you for that."

"I didn't do anything. Except make sure you got a decent meal. Have you been eating?"

"Sort of. Sam's been after me about it. I just haven't felt much like eating."

"I know, darlin'. Everything's going to be all right, no matter what happens. I'll make it all right. But you have to do your part to keep your body strong."

"You're right." She nodded. "I will."

"Good. Or I might have to get nasty with you."

Dusty couldn't help smiling at him. "In that case, I may have to starve myself."

Zach shook his head, and his lips curled into that wicked grin that stole Dusty's breath. "You're so damned adorable. So damned perfect."

"Sweetheart?"

"Hmm?"

"Since I now have no secrets from you, could you tell me something?"

He sighed. "You want to know the whole sordid Angelina story, don't you?"

"Mmm hmm."

"Are you sure? It's long and boring and I come off bad in it."

"I can't imagine you coming off bad in anything. Although what you ever saw in that Mary Ann Summers clone is beyond me."

"Who the hell is Mary Ann Summers?"

"From *Gilligan's Island*? Geez, Zach, don't you ever watch old reruns?"

"Mary Ann? The girl next door from Kansas? Heck, she's

hot." His tone was teasing.

"Don't get any ideas about dumping me for Angelina, *darlin'*."

Zach let out a guffaw. "Believe me, you have nothing to worry about."

"Then tell me the saga of the McCrays and the Bays."

"They own the ranch adjacent to ours."

"I thought Angelina said they were on the western slope."

"They are. That's Bay Crossing. But they also own a couple thousand acres that Angie's ma inherited from an uncle. They live there now. Angie and Harper went to high school in Bakersville. Angie was in Chad's class."

"Was she after you then?"

"Heck no. She was too young, and I already told you I didn't have any luck with girls in high school."

"I still don't understand that."

"I was all arms and legs, darlin'. Didn't fill out till later. Plus my eyes."

"I love your eyes."

"I'm glad. But most girls were just freaked out by them. I remember a certain little golden-haired tomboy who didn't much like them."

"Because you told me they'd melt my brain, you big bully!"

"Touché, darlin'. Anyway, Angie's ma and my ma became good friends and decided it would be a really great thing to combine the two ranches. Well, neither my pa nor Angie's would think about selling or partnering, so the women decided to push Angie and me together. This was a couple years ago."

"Why you?"

"Dallas was already married to Chelsea, and Chad was involved with someone else then."

"And?"

"And I wasn't seeing anyone at the time, and neither was she, so we decided to give it a try."

"Were you attracted to her at all?"

"She's a pretty girl. Not as hot as Mary Ann," he teased. "We found out later the scheme wouldn't have worked. Although I'd inherit my third of McCray Landing, Angie wouldn't get her ranch. It will go to Harper. Angie and her sister Caitlyn will jointly inherit Bay Crossing, the one on the western slope."

"Angie's mother didn't know any of this?"

"Nope."

"But it was her ranch."

"Owned jointly with her husband. Some men don't confide in their wives."

"Will you?"

"Darlin', you'll know everything that I do. Which sometimes is precious little."

"So what happened? Why did Angelina break up with you?"

"She said she didn't think I loved her."

"Did you?"

"No."

"So that's how you come off bad in the story. You were willing to marry a woman you didn't love."

"I didn't know what I was missing. I never loved anyone until you. Angie and I, we got along all right, and our mothers are so close, it just seemed the thing to do. I had affection for her."

"You were willing to spend your life without love?"

"Why not? I didn't know any better." He grinned at her. "I do now."

"Did she love you?"

"She claims she did. I don't think so though. I think she only wanted to start things up again because her biological clock is ticking and she doesn't have any other prospects at the moment."

"Oh." Dusty looked at her lap. That spark of hope she'd been feeling flickered and died.

"Jesus, I'm sorry. I didn't mean to bring that up."

"It's okay. At least that's one thing I don't have to worry about."

"What?"

"My biological clock, of course. What a load off my mind." She put her elbows on the table and buried her face in her hands.

"Come on, darlin'." Zach quickly signed the credit card receipt and stood up. He helped Dusty to her feet and brought her hand to his lips. The bristly brush of his beard against her skin comforted her. "You're the only woman I want, biological clock or no. Let's go home and make love all night."

When they got home, Dusty wanted to check on Jemma and the kittens, so she and Zach headed for the barn. One of the kittens was having trouble nursing. His mouth was slightly deformed and he couldn't latch on. It had been many hours since the kittens had been born, so he was near starving.

"Is there a vet you can call?" Zach asked.

"She's out of town," Dusty said. "I'm sorry, sweetheart. I'll have to take care of him tonight."

"We'll take care of him," Zach said. "But I have to tell you, I'm clueless. Chad would know what to do, but I always stayed away at birthing time."

"I don't have any cat formula, so he'll have to make do

with cow's milk. We'll dilute it and warm it up and then drop it on his tongue with a syringe. He'll have to sleep in the bedroom with us."

"The more the merrier." Zach curved his lips into his adorable grin.

Dusty smiled back, cradling the kitten in her arms. "Come on. We'll make a bed for him and feed him, and once he's settled, I'm all yours."

But Nigel, as Dusty had named the kitten, turned out to be high maintenance. It took Dusty over two hours to get him fed and settled, and she was exhausted when she finally joined Zach in bed. He kissed her, told her he loved her, and cradled her in his arms, where she stayed until the kitten wailed for her again.

★ ★ ★

Watching Dusty care for the helpless kitten throughout the night, Zach fell in love with her all the more. He vowed to make her a mother. Somehow. He couldn't remember the last time he'd prayed, but he did so now, silently pleading for Dusty's life. If things didn't go right, how would he live without her?

When Dusty crawled back into bed shortly before dawn after nursing the kitten once more, she climbed on top of Zach.

"Are you awake?" she asked.

"Yeah."

"I'm sorry I've kept you up all night."

"Darlin', I'm so happy to be here with you. I couldn't give a damn about sleep."

"In that case..." Dusty lifted off her T-shirt.

Zach sucked in his breath at the sight of her breasts falling gently. This woman would take his breath away for the rest of his life. He hardened instantly.

"I was determined to leave you alone," he said.

"I thought you wanted to make love all night."

"I did, but you've been up all night tending to the cat. I didn't want to bother you."

"You're hardly a bother." She lowered her head and twirled her tongue around his nipple. She feathered tiny kisses over his chest, up his neck, and nuzzled his Adam's apple. "Zach?"

"Hmm?"

"Promise me something."

"Anything."

"Well, I don't know how much time I'll have."

"Hush, darlin'. You're going to have lots of time."

"I hope so, but..."

"What?"

"I don't want to waste a precious second of it. Promise me we'll always make love. At least once every day."

"I think I can make that promise." He grinned.

"I'm serious." She caressed his cheeks lightly, ran her finger over his lips and over the edge of his beard. "No matter how tired we are. Or even if we're angry with each other. It's important..."

"Darlin', I'd make love with you twenty-four-seven if I could, and I'll never be so angry with you that I won't love you. I promise. I'll always desire you."

"Even when I'm bald?" She winced, her face contorting.

He took her hands in his and brought them both to his lips, kissing each individual finger. "You'll never be anything but beautiful to me. You're the sun and the moon. You're everything, Dusty. Everything. My whole world. I will always want to make love with you."

Her smile lit up her face like the morning sunrise peeking through the window. She scrambled out of her bikini panties and impaled herself on him. Already wet, she hugged him with sweet suction.

"Love me," she said, sliding up and down on his cock.

"I do. I do." He reached for her breasts and tugged gently on her nipples, relishing her sighs and whispers.

She made love to him slowly, provocatively, telling him how much she loved him with each sweet stroke. He savored the closeness, savored her, holding back, enjoying the sweet caresses of her snug sex against his cock. When he couldn't wait any longer, he reached down and thumbed her softly. Her climax came, and he let himself go and spilled into her, offering her his heart, his soul.

"I love you, Dusty," he said.

He held her close and prayed again.

CHAPTER EIGHTEEN

When dawn broke a little while later, Zach got up and helped Sam with the chores so Dusty could sleep. He attempted to feed Nigel but didn't have much luck. The tiny kitten squalled and cried until Dusty finally woke up.

"What are you doing to that poor thing?"

"I'm sorry, darlin'. I didn't want to wake you."

"It's all right. Look at the time. I need to help Sam with the chores."

"Already done." Zach smiled. "He and I took care of it. I wanted you to sleep."

"You're an angel."

"Just the man who loves you. But I'm afraid I'm not having much luck with Nigel here."

"I'm coming."

Dusty rose, her peachy naked body a tempting sight for Zach. He willed himself to cool off while she pulled on a pair of sweat pants and a tank top. That woman could make army fatigues look sexy. He handed the kitten to Dusty and kissed her lips. "I'll go get you some coffee."

"That'd be perfect. Thanks."

Zach walked to the kitchen, poured a cup of coffee for Dusty, and checked his watch. Only a little after nine. So he was startled when the phone rang. Sam was still outside, and Dusty made no move to answer it. He picked it up and said hello.

"Hello. Is this Sam?"

"Nope. Sorry. He's outside. I'll get him for you."

"No, no. I'm calling for Dusty, actually. This is Dr. Lloyd."

Zach's heart thumped against his sternum. "Oh, yeah, yeah. I'll get her for you. She's just in the next room. Hold on."

He ran to the bedroom, neglecting to put down the coffee so it sloshed all over his jeans. "Dusty." He took a deep breath, handing her the phone. "Dr. Lloyd."

Dusty put Nigel down on his bed and shakily reached for the phone. "Zach," she whispered.

"I'm here, darlin'." He sat down on the bed and pulled her into his lap. "We face it together, okay?"

She nodded and pressed the phone to her ear. "Good morning, Dr. Lloyd."

Zach felt Dusty tense on his lap. His own body was wound tighter than a bowstring. Why didn't she say something? How long did it take a doctor to say yes, you have cancer or no, you don't?

She sat, rigid, her eyes and mouth revealing nothing to him. A lone tear fell. Shit.

"It's okay, darlin'," he whispered. "We'll get through it."

Then, "What?" She dropped the phone onto the floor. Zach reached for it and put it back to her ear.

"I'm sorry, Doctor," she said. "Could you repeat that, please?" A pause. "Are you absolutely sure?" Another pause. "But how?"

Zach's mind whirled with jumbled thoughts of illness and loss as he imagined the absolute worst. Up until now he hadn't actually considered that he could lose Dusty. But now... He didn't want to live without her. He wasn't sure he could. Damn it, they would beat this!

"Thank you, Doctor. I appreciate you calling me so

quickly. You can't imagine what you've done for me. Thank you!"

She tossed the phone on the bed and then took Zach's mouth with hers. His heart hopped. Maybe it was good news. He broke away.

"What is it? Tell me."

She smiled, a wide smile he had never seen before. Always before, something had been clouding her smile. Now she was letting the sun itself shine through her. "It's wonderful news."

"I'm sitting on pins and needles here."

"I'm all right. My blood test came back normal."

"Thank God. What about the elevated white count earlier?"

"I was fighting a cold or something. Totally normal."

"Yee haw!" Zach stood up with her in his arms and swung her around. "Everything's going to be fine now. We're going to Colorado to start our life."

"Yes, we sure are."

"See? You were feeling sick because of nerves. Or maybe even a little virus."

"Or maybe a little something else." She smiled impishly.

"What have you got up your sleeve, darlin'?"

"Nothing up my sleeve. Just a little something in my belly. Do you still want to marry me today?"

"You bet I do. Just name the time and the place."

"As soon as possible. Unless you want our child to be born out of wedlock. I'm pregnant, Zach."

For the first time in his life, Zach McCray was speechless.

★ ★ ★

Zach's face was a shocked white. Wasn't he happy?

"Sweetheart, are you all right?"

He shook his head. "Fine, darlin'. Fine. But how?"

"Surely you don't need to ask that question. You certainly put a lot of effort into it."

He smiled sheepishly. "You know what I mean."

"Yeah, I know. I guess I'm not technically infertile. I do still get periods, just not very often. In order to get a period, I have to ovulate first. Evidently, I would have gotten a period right about now. Only you got to me first."

"But you were on the pill."

"No, I was never on the pill. You just assumed I was, and...I guess I let you believe it." *Oh God, what if he thought...*"I-I really didn't think I could get pregnant," she stammered, her face warming. "I never would have tried to trap you."

He cupped her cheeks and kissed her lips. "You don't have a deceptive bone in your gorgeous body, darlin'. I know you didn't mean to get pregnant. But I'm so damn glad you did. It's a miracle."

"Not a miracle. You're just a major stud who can impregnate an infertile woman." She kissed his cheek. "This is the most wonderful gift you could have ever given me."

"You're giving me the gift, darlin'. I'm so happy for you. For us. I'm not letting you out of my sight. I'm going to take such good care of you."

"You're going to smother me, aren't you?"

"Absolutely. No barrel racing and no roping. And especially no bull riding!"

"Zach—"

"I mean it, Dusty. This may be our only chance for a child."

"You're right, and I agree with you."

"You're acquiescing that easily? Where's my little spitfire?"

"Oh, she's still here. But she wants to have your baby more than anything in the world. I can't believe it, Zach. This is the happiest day of my life. I reached my five year mark. I'm cured. I'm in love, I'm getting married, and I'm having a baby." She began to cry.

"No crying allowed. You're happy, remember?"

"Oh, I am."

"Me too. More than ever."

"Zach, do you think he'll have your eyes?"

"God, I hope not."

"I hope so. Your eyes are so unique and wonderful. I love them. And I love you."

"I love you too, darlin'. Now let's get into Black Eagle and get hitched. I want to be your husband. And then we're heading straight home to McCray Landing. Your wedding gift is waiting there."

Dusty squealed. "Wedding gift? What have you done?"

"Not too much. Let's just say Harper Bay drives a hard bargain."

"Regina! Oh Zach! Now I have to get you something really special."

Zach smiled and rubbed his hand over her abdomen. "You already have, darlin'. You already have."

EPILOGUE

One year later

The beauty of the sun setting behind the Rocky Mountains never ceased to amaze Dusty. Vibrant hues of fuchsia and amethyst and then softer shades of lavender, rose, and tangerine. The Rockies themselves seemed translucent as the solar rays slowly faded and disappeared for another day. The redwood rocking bench on the front porch had been a gift from Zach when their son was born, and Dusty spent each evening there, enjoying the Colorado sunset.

Sean Jason McCray nursed urgently at his mother's breast. At three months old, he had more than doubled his birth weight, and he was thriving. Though born with a thick shock of dark hair, the peach fuzz growing in now was red-gold, like his mama's, and his eyes had turned light blue, the exact color of his daddy's left one.

"You're going to be a heartbreaker someday," Dusty cooed to him.

"That's a beautiful sight," Zach said as he came out the front door, his unique eyes reflecting the love that, to Dusty, seemed to grow stronger every day.

"You say that every evening." She smiled.

"It's a beautiful sight every evening, darlin'." He sat down beside her and stroked his son's soft head. He leaned down and kissed Dusty softly on the cheek. "Hey."

"Hey what?"

"Hey, I love you."

"I love you too, Zach."

"I have something to tell you. Two things, actually."

"What?"

"I've been doing some research."

"On what?"

"Oh, on colleges for my sweet, smart wife."

"Zach?"

"I want you to start taking classes this fall. The University of Central Colorado is only about an hour's drive from here. You can get your records transferred and get your degree in math and zoology. Then we'll see about vet school."

Dusty's heart leaped. Her wonderful husband would do anything to make her happy, but she had different dreams now. Different desires. Different goals.

"You're a sweetheart." She turned to kiss his soft lips. "But I don't want to leave Sean with a stranger. I want to be the one to raise my child, to put bandages on his scrapes and kiss them to make it better."

"But, darlin'—"

"Besides, the closest vet school is in Fort Collins, and I'd never leave here, so what's the point?"

"The point is that I don't want your brain to atrophy. You have an incredible intelligence, Dusty. You should use it."

"I will. Raising a child is the most important job in the world, and I plan to use my brain. Besides, you need my brain here. You know I can tend to the animals almost as well as any vet."

"True enough," Zach said, stroking her thigh. "Only if you're sure."

"I'm sure, and if I change my mind in the future, school

will still be there. Now what's the other thing you wanted to tell me?"

"I just got a phone call from Dallas."

"And?"

"He and Chelsea have separated, and he's filing for divorce."

"Oh, Zach, I'm so sorry."

"Hell, I'm not. The woman's a bitch." Zach cleared his throat. "Dallas and I have never been close. He was always such an overbearing know-it-all, but..."

"He's still your brother."

"Yeah. He's still my brother, and he deserves better than Chelsea." He smoothed the soft down on Sean's head. "He's been different since this little critter came along."

"He has. I think he really loves Sean. And he really loves you, Zach. He just wanted what was best for you."

"I have what's best for me." He kissed Dusty's cheek. "He knows that now. He's grown to love you, darlin'. Hell, anyone who gets to know you can't help but love you."

"I think you're a little bit biased."

"Nah." He sighed and stared straight ahead. "Beautiful sunset tonight."

"Isn't it?"

"More beautiful because I can share it with you and Sean." He grabbed a throw from the cedar table next to the bench and tucked it around the three of them.

Dusty smiled, the warmth in her heart flowing through her veins into every cell of her body. "We'll have many more sunsets together, sweetheart," she said.

They rocked silently as Sean nursed, and the soft darkness of the Colorado night enveloped them.

CONTINUE THE TEMPTATION SAGA WITH
BOOK TWO

Teasing

ANNIE

Available Now
Keep reading for an excerpt!

CHAPTER ONE

Dallas McCray was a little bit in love with his brother's wife.

Not in an "I have to have you" kind of way—though if they were both unattached he wouldn't kick Dusty out of bed—but more in an "I really wish I had someone like you to share my life with" kind of way.

He couldn't help thinking about his brother's happy marriage as he stared at the manila envelope he had just pulled from his mailbox.

His final divorce papers.

He took a deep breath and tore open the package. There it was in black-and-white. His marriage was over.

Not that he was upset about it. He no longer loved Chelsea. He wasn't sure he ever had, at least not in the way that Zach and Dusty loved each other. But failure was difficult for Dallas. Even the failure of a marriage he no longer wanted sliced like a hunting knife into his gut.

He strode into his home office, rolling his eyes at the thought of the colossal financial settlement he had paid Chelsea. Anything to keep from having to pay her alimony. He wanted her out of his life for good.

A clean break.

It had been easy enough. For Chelsea, it had always been about the money, and Dallas had plenty.

Thank God they hadn't had kids. Another knife cut into Dallas's heart at the thought of children. He had wanted them.

Chelsea hadn't. His face tensed at the memories of how she had deceived him.

Quickly he shoved the divorce papers into a file drawer. Best to get them out of sight.

So he didn't have children. Perhaps it wasn't meant to be. He was glad he hadn't had them with Chelsea, or he'd be bound to her for eternity. He'd probably be a terrible father anyway. His younger brothers had hated him growing up. They'd seen him only as an overbearing control freak, and he hadn't been close to either one. He was only now making reparations for his past actions toward them. Thankfully, they were both open to a new relationship with him.

On a whim, he picked up his cell phone and called Zach.

"What's up, Dallas?"

"They came today."

"The papers? You all right?"

"Yeah. I'm fine."

"Why don't you come to the house for dinner tonight? You shouldn't be alone."

"Nah. I'm okay."

"Come on. You know how Dusty loves to fuss over people. And Seanie misses his Uncle Dallas."

Dallas grinned as he thought of his one-year-old nephew. He did love that little guy, and letting Dusty fuss over him didn't sound too bad either.

"Deal," he said to Zach. "What time?"

"How's six-thirty sound? Seraphina's making spaghetti."

"Great." Dallas's mouth watered at the thought of zesty marinara. Zach and Dusty's housekeeper's Italian cuisine was legendary. "See you then."

★ ★ ★

Annie DeSimone yawned, stretching her bare arms over her head, her silver bangle bracelets clinking in her ears. Her first week as the new veterinarian in the small ranching town of Bakersville, Colorado was nearing its end, and already she had treated five horses, three cows, a stubborn bull, two dogs, and had delivered a litter of eight kittens.

To top it off, her VW Beetle had died on the way back from her last call, and she'd had to hitch a ride back to her office. Not a stellar first week, though at least the busyness had kept her mind off of other things.

Although it was only four, an hour before closing time, she walked to the door to lock up. As she flipped the sign from open to closed, a young woman walked around from the small parking lot behind the office, carrying a small child on one hip and an orange-and-white cat on the other.

"Geez," Annie said under her breath. She pasted a smile on her exhausted face and opened the door. "Hi," she said to the woman.

"You must be the new vet."

"Yes. I'm Dr. Annie DeSimone. Call me Annie. And you are?"

"Dusty McCray." She motioned to the pretty little boy who had striking light blue eyes and his mama's reddish-blond hair. "This is my son, Sean, and this"—she held up the cat—"is Nigel."

"It's nice to meet all of you," Annie said. She stroked Nigel's soft fur. "What seems to be the problem with Nigel today?"

"He's been lethargic for a few days," Dusty said. "Today,

though, he wouldn't eat anything at all, and his belly seems a little swollen. I think he might have a bowel obstruction." Dusty smiled nervously. "I'm afraid he likes to eat plastic wrap. We try to keep him away from it, but..."

"No need to explain. There's no keeping a curious cat from what he wants. The saying had to come from somewhere didn't it?"

"Saying?"

"Curiosity killed the cat, of course."

Dusty let out a small giggle. "I suppose so."

"But don't worry. Nigel's curiosity is only a small setback. Let's get him back on the table and have a look." Annie took the cat from his owner and led them to a small examining room. "All right, buddy, let's see what's going on." She set the cat down on the table and began her examination. "Has he vomited at all?"

"No," Dusty said.

"Any diarrhea?"

"Not that I've seen."

Annie palpated the cat's belly. "There's some distention here," she said, "but nothing too drastic. I don't think it's an obstruction. I think he may have eaten something that didn't agree with him."

Dusty sighed. "Yes, that's possible. The silly thing gets into everything."

Annie laughed. "Some cats are like that. If it would make you feel better, I can do a quick x-ray to definitely rule out an obstruction."

"Would you mind? Nigel is really special to me. I don't want to take any chances with him."

"Not at all. I'll need you to hold him down." She handed

Dusty a lead apron. "Is there any chance you might be pregnant?"

"No."

Annie showed Dusty how to position Nigel. "How would you like to come into the next room with me?" she asked Sean. "You can push the button."

Sean smiled and went willingly. *What a sweet little boy.*

After they had taken the picture, she took Sean back to his mother. "Why don't the two of you sit down out front and I'll be out in a few minutes. You can take Nigel with you."

Dusty nodded and led her son away.

Annie studied the digital image of the cat's abdomen. No obstruction, but he was a little constipated. Unusual for a cat, but not unheard of. She headed out front.

"Good news," she said. "As I suspected, there is no obstruction. He's a little backed up, though."

"Backed up?"

"Constipated."

"Oh." Dusty giggled. "I didn't know that could happen to cats."

"It can happen to any living creature," Annie said. "I'm going to give him a mild stool softener, and I suggest you keep him outside as much as you can for the next few days."

"Yes, of course."

"Don't hesitate to call if he gets worse," Annie said.

"I won't. Thank you so much. I know you were getting ready to close when I got here, and I really appreciate your time."

"No problem. I'm usually open till five, and of course I'm always on call for emergencies." She yawned. "It's been a harrowing week, though, and yes, I was tempted to close up early. But I'm glad I got to meet you and Sean and Nigel." She smiled.

"Have you met many people yet?"

"Only those whose animals I've treated. I've been hopping since I opened on Monday."

"Would you like to come to my house tonight for dinner?" Dusty asked. "It would give me a chance to repay you for your kindness, and I'd love for you to meet my husband."

A home-cooked meal sounded wonderful to Annie, who had subsisted on Lean Cuisines since she had opened up shop. "I'd love to come, but unfortunately my car died earlier today. I had it towed to Joe's down the street. I'm afraid I'm without transportation. Maybe some other time?"

"Don't be silly," Dusty said. "You can drive home with me right now, and Zach can drive you home later."

"I don't want to impose."

"You're not imposing. I'm the one who imposed on you late on a Friday afternoon when you were clearly trying to cut out early. Please. It would mean a lot to me."

"You're sure your husband won't mind?"

"Of course not."

"Well, then, I have to tell you, a home-cooked meal sounds absolutely divine."

"You'll love Seraphina's spaghetti," Dusty said. "Let's go." The pretty young woman offered a wide smile, which Annie returned.

She had made her first friend in Bakersville.

MESSAGE FROM HELEN HARDT

Dear Reader,

Thank you for reading *Tempting Dusty*. If you want to find out about my current backlist and future releases, please like my Facebook page: **www.facebook.com/HelenHardt** and join my mailing list: **www.helenhardt.com/signup/**. I often do giveaways. If you're a fan and would like to join my street team to help spread the word about my books, you can do so here: **www.facebook.com/groups/hardtandsoul/**. I regularly do awesome giveaways for my street team members.

If you enjoyed the story, please take the time to leave a review on a site like Amazon or Goodreads. I welcome all feedback.

I wish you all the best!

Helen

ALSO BY HELEN HARDT

The Sex and the Season Series:
Lily and the Duke
Rose in Bloom
Lady Alexandra's Lover
Sophie's Voice
The Perils of Patricia (Coming Soon)

The Temptation Saga:
Tempting Dusty
Teasing Annie
Taking Catie
Taming Angelina
Treasuring Amber
Trusting Sydney
Tantalizing Maria

The Steel Brothers Saga:
Craving
Obsession
Possession
Melt (Coming December 20th, 2016)
Burn (Coming February 14th, 2017)
Surrender (Coming May 16th, 2017)

Daughters of the Prairie:
The Outlaw's Angel
Lessons of the Heart
Song of the Raven

ACKNOWLEDGMENTS

The *Temptation Saga* is very special to me, and I'm grateful to Waterhouse Press for acquiring it and taking it to this new level. Formerly my *Bakersville Saga*, this series has had several incarnations, and the first four books in the series are award winners and/or finalists.

Tempting Dusty (formerly Ivy League Cowboy) is especially important to me, not only because it's the first book in the series and the most decorated—most notably winning the RomCon Readers' Crown Award in 2012—but also because the two main characters are named after the first two dogs I had as an adult. Dusty was a golden retriever, and Zach was half German Shepherd and half Husky...and yes, he had black hair and one brown eye and one blue eye!

So many people helped along the way in bringing this book to you. Celina Summers, Michele Hamner Moore, Jenny Rarden, Coreen Montagna, Kelly Shorten, David Grishman, Meredith Wild, Jonathan Mac, Kurt Vachon, Yvonne Ellis, Shayla Fereshetian—thank you all for your expertise and guidance.

And thanks most of all to you, the readers. I hope you love Zach and Dusty's story. Up next is Zach's brother Dallas, who meets his match in a feisty veterinarian from New Jersey. Don't miss *Teasing Annie!*

ABOUT THE AUTHOR

New York Times and *USA Today* Bestselling author Helen Hardt's passion for the written word began with the books her mother read to her at bedtime. She wrote her first story at age six and hasn't stopped since. In addition to being an award winning author of contemporary and historical romance and erotica, she's a mother, a black belt in Taekwondo, a grammar geek, an appreciator of fine red wine, and a lover of Ben and Jerry's ice cream. She writes from her home in Colorado, where she lives with her family. Helen loves to hear from readers.

Visit her here:
www.facebook.com/HelenHardt

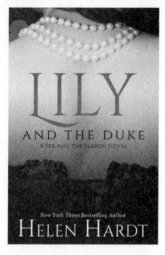

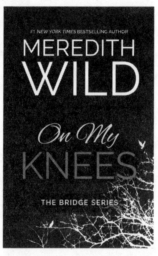